"With an accomplished hand, Les Daniels turns back the bloodstained pages of history to reveal new horrors, man-made and supernatural. A fearsome, fascinating glimpse of life and death—and the strange realm between."

—Robert Bloch

Sebastian's face appeared abruptly in the gloom. His flesh glowed with a pale blue light; the flame grew brighter until the features burned away and left only a gleaming silver skull. It spoke to her.

"What is worse than death?"

Then he was upon her. When it was over, Sebastian rose alone. Felicia lay at ease, her limbs sprawled in graceful carelessness, her face hardly tinged by shock.

When the next sun set, she would rise, full of dark desire.

His tears, when they came, were tinged with her bright blood.

YELLOW FOG

LES DANIELS

TOR
HORROR

A TOM DOHERTY ASSOCIATES BOOK

YELLOW FOG

A substantially different version of YELLOW FOG was published by Donald M. Grant, Publisher, Inc., and printed in 1986.

A TOR Book
Published by Tom Doherty Associates, Inc.
49 West 24 Street
New York, NY 10010

Cover art by Maren

ISBN: 0-812-51675-3   Can. ISBN: 0-812-51676-1

First edition: August 1988

Printed in the United States of America

0 9 8 7 6 5 4 3 2 1

Contents

PROLOGUE

1835

The little girl sat crumpled in her corner, frightened by the rattling speed of the train, and even more frightened by the face of her grinning, bearded father.

"Anything wrong with these rails?" demanded Horace Lamb.

Neither his wife nor his daughter answered him.

"Not a damned thing!" he insisted, and then he began to laugh, a sound so loud that it seemed to fill the entire first-class compartment, pushing Felicia back against the plush cushion of her seat. The mahogany armrest dug into her ribs. She tried to imagine that she was sitting in a chair at home, but the chairs at home didn't rattle, and they didn't shake, and they didn't rush through the night at more than thirty miles an hour. For an instant she had a vision that something like that might happen, that her family's sturdy brick house might go roaring through the streets of London the way this train ran down its track, and the picture in her mind dismayed her so much that she was actually relieved when her father shattered the image with the sound of his voice.

"Wrought iron indeed!" he snorted. "Do you realize how much more that would have cost the company for every foot of rail we laid? Can't expect to make money if you throw it away, can you? Cast iron's good enough, no matter what they say. Iron is iron."

"I'm sure you're right, my dear," said Mrs. Lamb. "I do wish, though, that we didn't have to travel in the nighttime."

Felicia would have agreed if she had dared, but the expression that came over her father's face made her glad she had kept silent.

Horace Lamb glared at his wife, then took hold of himself. She was only a woman, after all, and prone to fears and fancies. He patted her hand magnanimously.

"We have these oil lamps, don't we?" he said defensively. "Every modern convenience. And we didn't intend to travel at night, damn it, but there's always some delay when a new line opens. Trouble starting the engine. And we had to make the first run on the day we announced, or I'd become a laughingstock. You don't really mind, do you?"

"Of course not, Horace," said Mrs. Lamb. Felicia thought her mother's face looked white and strained beneath her bonnet. It bothered the girl when her mother looked like this, but it was a familiar sight.

"Good," said Mr. Lamb. "You know how important it is that you and the girl ride along with me on this maiden voyage. We must show all of England that traveling by rail is safe, even elegant. It's not enough to carry the mail, or goods, or livestock, when there's so much money to be made from passengers. A fortune to be made! And it's all for you and the child, you know. It may seem to you that we have plenty, but there's never enough, I assure you."

Felicia looked up at him nervously. "Aren't the cows afraid, riding in those open cars at night?"

"Of course not, Felicia," her mother said. "Animals are accustomed to living out of doors."

"They're only going to be killed anyway," her father said. Felicia cringed.

"I must say I do feel sorry for the people riding in the third-class carriages," said Mrs. Lamb. "They ride much like the cattle. No sides to their coaches. Not even a covering for

3

their heads as they might have if they could afford a second-class ticket."

"Then let 'em buy a second-class ticket," bellowed Mr. Lamb. "Or let 'em walk. They get what they pay for! Must I endure criticism from my own family, when everything I do is for their benefit? Must I?"

Everyone was silent, and Horace Lamb sat back, glowering but satisfied, a massive figure in the flickering light of the swaying oil lamp. The train bucked and bounced, its wheels rattling out a jagged rhythm against cast-iron rails.

Standing at the rear of his gleaming red and black steam locomotive, the driver clutched the throttle in one hand and his tall silk hat in the other. His coat was of the same color scheme as the engine, and so were the tiny red and black embers that it spat at him, constantly threatening to send his uniform up in flames. He nervously peered ahead into the darkness and cursed Horace Lamb at the top of his voice, confident that nothing could be heard over the roar of the pistons. It was madness to run at night, and the lantern that had been placed at the driver's feet did nothing to alleviate the blackness up ahead. He should have protested, but he knew it was more than his job was worth. He glanced backward and saw only the faint glow from the first-class carriages, but he could imagine the rest of the train: cars laden with coal and mail and cattle, and cars where human beings were packed like beasts.

The ten wheels of the locomotive, pushed by throbbing pistons, rolled down their flimsy tracks toward London. Had the driver known more about the construction of the line, he would have been more concerned with what was under his train than what might be in front of it, but as it was, his main concern was to put on more speed and bring this dark journey to a quick conclusion. The sooner they reached their destination, the sooner they would be safe. He pulled the bell rope, offering a warning to what he could not see, and strained his eyes for a glow ahead that might presage the lights of the city.

Mr. Horace Lamb was equally concerned to have the trip come to an end. A fast and efficient trip was a good selling point, and while there was no chance to set a record while traveling at night, a good time might do something to quiet the stockholders. He pulled a big gold watch from the pocket of his flowered silk waistcoat.

"Just a few more minutes," he announced. He smiled at his daughter in the mistaken belief that the sight of so many large and yellow teeth was reassuring.

"A few more minutes for what, sir?" Felicia asked timidly, half convinced that she was being threatened.

"Why, until the train stops," said her father, but in this, as in so many things, he was mistaken.

He was wrong, for instance, when he suggested that he had not made enough money to keep Felicia in comfort for the rest of her life. And he was wrong about the train, which stopped precisely seventeen seconds after he spoke, when a rail with a flaw in its core cracked under the pressure of the first wheel that touched it.

The locomotive ran off the tracks and plowed into the damp earth of England. It slid down a grassy slope and tipped slowly, ponderously, to one side.

The driver felt what he could not see. He was off balance, and the sensation was much like floating in an endless dream. He seemed to hang suspended in space for an eternity, his equilibrium gone, his mind perfectly concentrated yet oddly empty.

The lantern at his feet glided across the floor and out into the night, where it shattered and burst into flame. He floated after it, and was saved from a painful death by fire only when the locomotive gave a metallic groan and collapsed on top of him. He was crushed in an instant, still lost in his dream.

Unfortunately for his passengers, the metal that linked the carriages together was made of far sterner stuff than the rails. The weight and momentum of the falling engine pulled the cars forward and outward, one by one. The creaking couplings held long enough to topple each car in its turn. To something flying overhead, Horace Lamb's train would have looked like a row of tumbling dominoes.

And there was something overhead, a gargantuan shape whose vast wings beat against the blackness of the sky.

It had sensed the train before it heard the endless, roaring crash, before the fires had flared as if a writhing serpent, plump with fat, had been tossed onto a bed of flaming coals. It had sensed the life beneath it long before, seen in its mind's eye a rushing stream of blue and silver that ran through the dark land far below.

Here there was prey.

Wings wide, it soared in a slow spiral toward the wreckage, turning down and in upon itself like a dark whirlpool. At the bottom of the whirlpool there was blood.

The screams of men and women were almost lost beneath the frantic bellowing of frightened cattle. A bull emerged from the wreckage of one car, its back smoldering. It spotted the winged creature as it settled to the ground, and charged furiously toward it. The maddened bull, head lowered, was baffled by a change it saw only dimly as the winged thing before it seemed to dwindle down into the figure of a man. It would have been still more surprised, had it been granted the power of reason, when it felt the man's hands, startlingly strong, grasp it by the horns and twist its head around until it was ripped free. The decapitated beast sank down, bathing its assailant in hot blood.

The dark man moved toward the flames. Something moved at his feet: a whimpering, crawling worm that had been, only a moment before, a man. His name had been Peter Benson, and he was as good as dead. He had been journeying to London in the third-class carriage, which was all that he could afford, to visit his dying father, who would outlive him by several days. Peter Benson's right arm was gone, and he was losing more blood than he could afford.

He asked for help, and the man standing above him did all that he could do: He knelt beside Benson and cradled him in his arms; he stroked his hair and murmured "Peter;" he fastened his mouth to the bleeding stump where a strong right arm had been and drank until there was no more to drink.

As the dark man rose, he pulled off Benson's long, heavy coat to cover his own nakedness. His thirst was satisfied, but his curiosity was not. He drifted toward the train. Someone ran past him howling, entirely aflame. He wondered idly if it was a man or a woman.

Something drew him forward, a small spot of stillness in the midst of chaos. There was a speck of life in one of the overturned carriages, life that was full of shock and sorrow, and yet would not give way to fear.

With unnatural agility he climbed up the undercarriage of an overturned first-class coach, reached the top, which once had been a side, and wrenched open the door. He looked down into the dark.

A small, frail woman lay in one corner, her eyes and mouth round with surprise. A heavy, bearded man sprawled facedown beside her, smothering an oil lamp which had cut and burned into his stomach. There was no way to tell if this was accident or heroism.

Sitting across from them was a beautiful child with hair so pale that it was almost white. Her hands were folded, and a broken beam of wood had wedged itself above her so that she could not rise. She seemed to be waiting for something.

Felicia Lamb looked up and saw a man

whose long black hair fell all around his thin white face.

"They're dead, aren't they?" she said. "They've gone to heaven. I'd like to go to heaven too, but you see I can't get out."

"Do you wish to be free?" the man asked her.

She nodded gravely.

"So do I," he said.

He slithered through the opening above her and grasped the beam of wood in both his hands, and where he touched it, the wood crumbled into sawdust. He pulled her free and held her close to him.

"Will you take me to heaven now?" she asked. "I'm afraid of the other place."

"So are we all," he said.

He gathered her up and carried her out into the night, away from the sour smoke and the flickering flames and the shouts and groans and cries. He brought her to where it was cool and quiet, to an empty field where there was nothing to be seen but the small cold stars dotting a vast and empty sky. His coat slipped from his shoulders; his long fingers gently closed her eyes.

"Sleep, Felicia," he said.

She felt him tremble. He spun her around as if they were dancing, and then she felt the ground drop away beneath her. The wind from his great wings caressed her face, and she knew she was in the arms of an angel.

Felicia was too prudent to look the angel in the face, but nonetheless she opened her eyes, and the world she saw was wonderful.

She soared through space with the dark man. The sky was full of spinning lights as bright and beautiful as diamonds. As he carried her to even greater heights, she saw another sky of lights below: the lights of life, the lights of London. And each one of these, the lights of heaven and the lights of earth, was the sign of a spirit, and there were spirits everywhere.

Felicia swooned in ecstasy.

The next morning she was found sleeping on the doorstep of her father's home. Her relatives fussed over her, especially her spinster aunt Penelope, and they wondered how she had wandered so far from the scene of the tragedy that had killed so many, so many miles away. They spoke knowingly of the strength within each of us, and how a crisis brought it to the fore. To spare the child they did not speak to her at all.

And so it was that no one knew (except Felicia Lamb) that Death himself had carried her away and brought her safely home.

O N E

A Chair by
the Window

Mr. William Callender, almost eighty and feeling every year of it, lounged in an over-stuffed brown leather chair and dozed behind his copy of *The Times*. He'd read the date, November 9, 1847, but hadn't really tried to read much more; the news was never good anyway, and the type the paper used seemed to shrink with every issue. Not even his small gold-rimmed spectacles helped very much these days. He let them slip down his nose, draped the newspaper over his expensive paunch, and settled back into the luxurious piece of furniture which was his by something very much like divine right.

He was, after all, the oldest living member of the Commerce Club.

Doubtless there were other chairs as good, but this one stood by the bay window that overlooked Pall Mall, where there was entertainment to be had in the sight of people hurrying about on business when he himself had none. Furthermore, the warmth of the sunshine was very pleasant here, at least in the summer months, even if the weak gray light of this fall day was cold comfort at best. Still, the principal advantage of this most desirable of chairs was its position in a remote nook of the club library, set apart from the forced congeniality of the rest of the room. No need here for a nod or a greeting, and few indeed were the members with the audacity to approach Old Callender at his repose.

One of the few, of course, who would consider it was Young Callender—his nephew Reginald. Having one's own relatives on the premises was even more disturbing than the presence of the inevitable club bore, a Mr. Winter. It had probably been worth it, Callender decided, to have sponsored the last remaining member of his family for membership here, yet in a sense it defeated the whole purpose of a club, which was to provide a pleasant refuge from such burdens as family, friends, females, and finance. Here one was entitled, for a fee, to be left entirely alone. As it was, however, young Reginald was a continuing source of irritation, not the least because he clearly expected to inherit this chair along with his uncle's fortune. Mr. William Callender, in point of fact, had little interest in relinquishing either of these luxuries.

Reginald puzzled him. It was not that the boy was a rake, as such fellows had been called when he himself was young, but that he was so little else. It was natural for a young man to spend at least part of his time in drinking, gaming, and wenching; that was part of a liberal education. But was there nothing more to life?

Old Callender thought back to his own youth, when the Commerce Club was no more than a group of clever youngsters who met once a week to discuss their prospects in trade, manufacture, and investment. It had proved to be a beneficial association, especially regarding advice on shares in the East India Company, but none among their number could have imagined then that it would lead in time to the elegant building that housed them now. An edifice to the privileges and perquisites of successful men, the Commerce Club opened its doors to no one who had not made his own way in the world, except, of course, for Reginald Callender. Yet there might be time for the boy to do something with himself, his uncle William thought, especially now that

he was about to be married. The girl was
certainly suitable; in fact, the old man had
selected her himself. In any case, there was
more to be gained from sleep than from
brooding about the future.

Old Callender had just sunk into that deli-
cious state, halfway between waking and
dreaming, which his long years had taught
him was one of the greatest pleasures that life
affords, when he was jolted back into the
curse of consciousness by a rasping, nasal,
high-pitched voice. He didn't need to open his
eyes to know that he had fallen victim to
Winter, the club bore.

"Have you seen this, Callender?" Winter
sounded like a man with much on his mind.

"I have seen nothing, my dear fellow. My
eyes, as you perceive, have been completely
closed."

"Well, you must hear it, then. It's an attack
on you. On me. On all of us!"

Old Callender slowly raised one eyelid and
beheld his tormentor in all his red-haired,
round-faced, rabbity indignation.

"You interest me strangely," said Callender.
"What's that you're waving at me?"

"This! This is what I'm talking about."

"It looks to me like an issue of Hood's
Comic Annual."

"That's just the point! Some woman has

written a poem or some such thing denouncing the institution of clubs for men. She says that we're destroying the family and the home. And this fellow Hood has printed it! Listen."

Callender let his eye shut again. He sighed audibly as Winter began his recital, droning on for ten full verses while Callender felt his face turn hot and red. He cursed inwardly at his cravat and the man who had invented it. The only use that such an instrument should have was to be tightened around Winter's neck until he choked like a chicken. And in truth his voice did seem to be rising into a cackling scream as he reached the climax of his oration:

> *Of all the modern schemes of Man*
> *That time has brought to bear,*
> *A plague upon the wicked plan,*
> *That parts the wedded pair!*
> *My wedded friends they all allow*
> *They meet with slights and snubs,*
> *And say, "They have no husbands now,*
> *They're married to the Clubs!"*

The club bore paused dramatically for effect, and Old Callender sensed rather than saw that heads had turned all over the library at the sight and sound of such a display. It

17

followed that his own time was ripe.

"I think you take this all too much to heart," he began. "After all, there are clubs of many kinds, are there not?"

"To be sure—" Winter began, but Callender cut him off.

"And what might apply in one club would not apply in another. The Commerce Club is composed of sober and serious men of affairs. Many of us, like myself, have never married. No doubt there are clubs of other types. Some of them, I believe, admit poets, and even actors." He took a deep breath, then thundered out, "And if you insist upon reciting verse, I strongly suggest you join one of them!"

Winter gasped and backed away to the accompaniment of muffled laughter from all around the library, and the club's oldest member sat back in its most honored seat, somewhat more agitated than he had expected to be. He felt a vein throb in his forehead, and it acclerated into a twitch when he glanced out the window and spotted his nephew Reginald making his way across Pall Mall and toward the entrance to the Commerce Club.

It did nothing to improve Old Callender's temper to notice that his nephew was decked out in a handsome new suit of pale gray, complete with a matching high silk hat. Unlike Reginald, his uncle was not a betting man, but he would have been more than willing to wager that the suit had been charged to his own account. And however fashionable a figure Reginald cut, with his new clothes and his sandy side whiskers, his uncle was not pleased by his presence, which was certain to cost him money in one way or another. The vein in his forehead squirmed like a snake. This was insufferable. He decided to see if he could leave undetected, even though that would mean sneaking out of his own club like a common thief, but when he tried to rise, he experienced yet another unpleasant surprise.

Reginald Callender, a bit hung over but not really distressed by it, took the steps of the Commerce Club at a brisk rate and waved cheerfully to the doorman as he walked in. Even with a mild headache life was good. Just to enter this splendid institution was a source of considerable satisfaction to him. This was what he deserved; this was where he belonged.

The huge vacant hall that received all who entered the club had a floor of marble mosaic; situated around the walls were massive white pillars whose purpose, if any, was more decorative than functional. In the center of the hall was a life-size statue of a bearded man whose inscribed name Young Callender didn't recognize; he had never been concerned enough to ask anyone who it might be. Behind the bronze figure, above the ornate fireplace, hung a painting of someone he did recognize: the Queen. Flanking her on either side were the two entrances to the strangers' dining room, the area where members were permitted to entertain their guests. The floors above were sacrosanct.

Callender hesitated before the great fireplace. A bite of food might be in order, since he couldn't recall having dined since last night, and he wasn't even certain about that. On the other hand, the company in the dining room was always an open question; he would probably be better served by a few drinks and a few friends in the billiards room. He might even be able to scare up a little ready money, thus postponing the necessity of putting the bite on his uncle William.

He strolled to the elaborate wrought iron staircase, his ebony walking stick rattling against the railings as he ascended past prints of ships and trains and factories and other emblems of industry. They did not interest him.

At the head of the stairs he turned down a narrow, dimly lit hallway. At its end, from behind an oaken door, he heard the sound of laughter.

The air in the billiards room was aromatic with spicy smoke from a good fire and pipes of Turkish tobacco. Two men lounged by the table, their game just completed, while three others sat around the fireplace giving their orders to a liveried waiter. Callender strode into the room and dropped his hat and stick into an empty chair.

"Good afternoon, gentlemen. A fine day for a brandy. And a better day for a large one," he told the waiter. "This round will be mine."

"Yours, sir, Mr. Callender?"

"Am I slurring my words? Is my tongue thick? It seems too early in the day for that!" Callender smiled, but not pleasantly.

The waiter gave him a nervous look, bowed, and scurried out the door. Callender glanced around.

"What do you say to a game, Dickson? Five guineas?"

"I say you haven't got five guineas, and you'll just be deeper in my debt if I'm fool enough to play with you."

The words were delivered with the same sort of smile Callender had offered the waiter, and it was no more convincing. Callender's face grew pale. He tried to stare down Dickson, a man he had always envied and disliked. He was only a few years older than Callender and in all externals equally idle, but he had capital, as well as investments that always seemed to bring returns. That was bad enough, but now his manner was becoming positively condescending.

"Are you implying something?" Callender asked coldly.

"Surely not," said one of the men by the table.

"No, of course not," said Dickson. "Do sit down, Callender. I'm sure your credit's good. Your prospects are certainly excellent. I was just wondering whether it would be your uncle or the girl you plan to marry who would end up paying for that large brandy. . . ."

"You leave Miss Lamb's name out of this," barked Callender.

"Here now," said the man by the table, rushing forward to plant his substantial bulk between Dickson and Callender. "No arguments, gentlemen. And no talk of ladies. You're quite out of line, Dickson, if I do say so."

Everyone in the room was perfectly still. The only sound came from the crackling fire.

"You're quite right, Palmer," Dickson finally said. "I've been in a foul temper all day. I heard this morning that a ship was lost, one I'd backed. I don't know how many thousands it cost me. Still, there it is. And it's no excuse for discourtesy. You must forgive me, Callender."

"Of course he does," said Palmer affably. "There's not a better fellow in the Commerce Club than Reggie Callender."

"Yes," said Callender at length. "Think nothing of it, Dickson. Sorry about your ship."

Dickson sat brooding into the fire.

"Come on, Young Callender," boomed Palmer, "you have a game with me. And we won't even discuss payment, because you're certain to beat me. Ah, look. Here are those drinks at last."

Callender snatched his brimming snifter off the tray and downed it in a gulp. He'd been furious with Dickson, of course, but it was almost worth it to receive an apology while simultaneously learning that his tormentor had suffered a substantial loss. He picked up a cue and was eyeing it carefully in the flickering light, when the waiter sidled up to him.

"I beg your pardon, sir," said the man in a stage whisper. "I hate to disturb you, but it's your uncle, sir."

"My uncle? What about him?"

"My message is that he must see you at once, sir. Would you be good enough to follow me?"

A dozen thoughts flickered through

Reginald Callender's mind, none of them pleasant. He was rarely summoned except to be called on the carpet, yet he was guilty of so many petty infractions that he could hardly guess which one might have inspired his uncle's latest bout of indignation. It might be anything. It might even be the very clothes he wore. The suit. That was it for a certainty. No doubt the old boy had been in his damned seat by the window and had spotted the offending garment as it passed into the club. For a moment Reginald was tempted to bunk it. He had no wish to experience a dressing down, but it would have to come sooner or later, and the truth was that Uncle William's lectures often shamed the giver as much as the receiver, to the point where they were frequently followed by the offer of some very welcome pocket money. At any rate, there wouldn't be much shouting or pounding of fists on tables in the sanctuary of the club library. Perhaps the summons was a godsend.

"You'll have to excuse me for a moment, gentlemen. My uncle needs me. A matter of business, no doubt. I'll return as soon as I can."

The waiter followed him out into the hallway, as if there could be any doubt about his uncle's location, or about the way to the library.

"Please, sir. You needn't bother going in there."

"What are you talking about, man? You just told me, only a few seconds ago—"

"Yes, sir. I know, sir, but that was what we call a subterfuge. A ruse, sir. We don't like to embarrass gentlemen if we can help it, sir. . . ."

Callender stopped in his tracks and turned on the man. "What the devil are you babbling about?"

"Well, sir, the fact is, sir, it isn't your uncle who wants to see you at all. It's the club steward. He says something has to be done about your bill. Of course I brought that last round you ordered, sir. I wouldn't dream of saying nothing in front of the other gentlemen. But the club steward, Mr. Frayling, he says it's coming out of my pay if your accounts aren't settled. And it was six brandies, sir!"

Reginald Callender's scowl relaxed into something very like a smile. He pushed his right hand through his sandy hair. This might be a jolt, but hardly an unfamiliar one.

"That was quite decent of you, and I promise you won't regret it. There'll be quite a handsome tip for you as soon as things are settled. So I'm posted, am I?"

"That's right, sir. Posted."

"Don't you worry. It's all a mistake. I'll have

a word with Frayling right away. Is he in his cubbyhole?"

"Yes, sir. Up above, sir."

"Thank you. I know the way."

Callender strode down the hall toward another stairway. This would have to be attended to at once.

The floor above, like the basement with its vast kitchen, was principally given over to the workings of the Commerce Club. Here were offices, quarters for some of the servants who were expected to be on beck and call at any hour of the night, and also palatial rooms for the few members who sometimes found it peaceful or otherwise convenient to spend the night away from home.

And here, like a spider in its lair, sat Frayling, the club steward. He was not a member, and would never have been allowed to be, yet in a sense he ruled the Commerce Club, for he had been engaged to supervise its every operation, and that included the keeping of the books. Callender strongly suspected that Frayling's greatest pleasure came from the occasional opportunity to shame one of his betters who had run up a substantial debt. As Callender pushed open the small plain door, he promised himself that as soon as he had the power and money that he expected, he would do what he could to have the man dismissed.

The tiny room was unadorned except for the rows of ledgers that stood behind the small man seated at his desk. Another ledger, this one open, rested on the desktop.

"Look here, Frayling," Callender began.

"Ah! Mr. Callender! I was expecting you."

"What's this about posting me?"

"That was my duty, Mr. Callender. A most unpleasant one to be sure. But I have my obligation to the other members, and you are so far in arrears that I fear I can no longer offer you the privileges of a member." Frayling shook his small head sadly, but his eyes looked positively merry.

"So," said Callender. "How much is it, then?"

The steward held up his ledger and pointed to a number written there. His victim bent down to read it. He noticed that Frayling's finger shook, and wondered if it was from nervousness or laughter.

"As much as that?" asked Callender, his eyes wide. "That must have taken months!"

"That's my point, Mr. Callender. And since neither you nor your uncle has seen fit to pay anything . . ."

"And is my uncle behind like this too?"

27

"On the contrary, his accounts are quite up-to-date. He generally pays cash, I believe."

Callender stood silent for a minute. "I'll attend to this," he finally said. "There must be some mistake. An oversight. I'll be back directly."

"I am always here to serve the members," said Frayling pointedly, closing his ledger as Callender closed the door.

As Callender headed down the steps toward the library, he wondered if there had been an oversight at all. He would not put it past his uncle to have done this deliberately, yet another of his pointless but infuriating efforts to provide a lesson on the value of money. Now there would be a lecture for sure, but Callender would be glad to hear it if it could ensure that at least this one debt would be paid at once. To be barred from the Commerce Club was unthinkable.

He hardly knew how he would approach his uncle. The anger he felt could hardly be expressed if he hoped to achieve his end, yet the feeling surging in him made some sort of action an absolute necessity. He walked through the entrance to the library.

The room was still and dim in the light of the November afternoon. No lamps had been lit, and everything seemed gray. Something sent a chill into Callender. There seemed to be nobody in the library, nothing but shadows and silence. His uncle might be gone, and Callender obliged to follow him, in which case there was a chance, however unlikely, that he would never be permitted to enter the hallowed halls of the club again.

Suddenly afraid, he tiptoed toward the nook where his uncle usually sat, next to the bay window that overlooked Pall Mall. His feet made no sound on the thick carpet. He held his breath. He approached the back of the oldest member's brown leather chair.

And then he heard something that caused him to sigh with audible relief. It was a rasping, snorting, gurgling sound, and one that he recognized. It was the sound of his uncle William snoring.

Callender moved to the front of the chair, blocking out what little light there was. What he saw in the chair, however dimly, was not what he expected. His uncle was there, sure enough, but his eyes were open, and they rolled desperately at the sight of his nephew. What might have been snoring now sounded more like choking. The old man's face looked nearly purple, and a trickle of saliva ran down his chin. A pool of it had formed on his shirtfront. He seemed to be trying to get out of his chair, but he kept falling back again. Only one of his arms was working.

Callender staggered back from the chair in shock. He had no idea what to do.

He stood frozen for a moment, then turned and ran across the library floor. He tripped over a footstool and stumbled to the door. He couldn't make the knob work, began to panic, then burst through into the narrow hallway and staggered down the stairs.

He stood in the vast marble hall that marked the entrance to the club, his shouts echoing among the pillars.

"Help! Someone! Anyone! Get a doctor! It's my uncle! William Callender! He's had some sort of seizure!"

His voice called back to him from the empty hall, and not even Callender himself could have said if he cried out in terror or in triumph.

T W O

Patience

The glass jar was filled with things that squirmed.

Felicia Lamb stared at them in shock and surprise, then turned away when she realized what they were. Dr. Franklin put the jar on the nightstand beside William Callender's canopied bed and rummaged through his black leather bag in search of other medical supplies. A candle's flame made dark silhouettes of the shapes that twisted in pale liquid, sending their shadows across the dim bedchamber to fall upon Felicia and the wall behind her. She reached out for her aunt Penelope's small, strong fingers.

Dr. Franklin pushed aside the curtains that covered his patient's bed and held up the candle in one trembling hand. He was hardly younger than the man stretched out before him, whom he had known for more than forty years. A glance was enough to convince him that he would probably not know the man for a great deal longer.

Propped up on a mountain of pillows, with the blankets tucked up under his chin, Franklin's old friend already looked disturbingly like the specimen of a severed head on display for the edification of medical students. The head was large and round, but the fleshy cheeks and jowls seemed to have collapsed upon themselves. Their color was mottled, either too dark or too light for a good prognosis. The eyes were unfocused, and one of them was bloodshot; they seemed to look in opposite directions. A wet cloth was draped across the forehead; Dr. Franklin removed it gently and used it to wipe the spittle from his patient's lips and chin.

"Who did this?" he demanded, holding up the dripping cloth.

"It was I," Felicia answered in a trembling voice. "Did I do wrong? I thought there might be a fever, and he seemed to be suffering, poor man, even if he couldn't speak to say what troubled him."

"No harm done. A cold compress is good for many ailments, that's a fact. But not for this one, I'm afraid."

"Will it hurt him?"

"No, miss, I didn't mean that at all. You may even have given him some comfort. But it will take more than that to cure him. He's had a cerebral hemorrhage, I should say, a broken blood vessel in the brain, and there's not much we can do for that."

"Why, you haven't even examined him!" protested Aunt Penelope.

Dr. Franklin turned his gaze on her. She was a tiny, birdlike woman whose graying hair showed her age while her unlined face concealed it. Her eyes were bright and inquisitive.

"We both knew this was coming," he told her, "both Mr. Callender and I. The pressure of his blood was too strong, the veins and arteries too weak. It was bound to happen sooner or later. You may be sure that I will examine him, but I expect to find my diagnosis confirmed, and in that case there's little enough I can do for him. A careful bleeding might provide some small relief."

"Can he hear what we're saying?" asked Felicia Lamb.

"Don't know," admitted Dr. Franklin as he glanced at the young woman. Her golden hair was almost as pale as her face, and her blue eyes were wide as they sought the jar on the table. Her figure, beneath a simple gray dress that buttoned up almost to her chin, was

33

graceful but decidedly frail. Dr. Franklin made another snap diagnosis and decided that she had no place in the sick room. Her aunt, though, looked peppery and competent; she might have been a nurse, and she could prove useful. He turned to her niece.

"You're betrothed to the nephew, are you?"

Felicia nodded, adding half a curtsy and more than half a blush.

"Well, then, you'd better see to him. He's downstairs, quite distracted, sitting with a bottle of brandy and playing that game with a pack of cards, the one that people play alone . . . I don't know what it's called."

"Patience," said Aunt Penelope with a sniff.

"Just so," said Dr. Franklin. "Well, young miss, I'll ask you to go down and stay with him, if you'll be so kind. He needs you now much more than we do."

"Just as you say, Dr. Franklin." Felicia moved across the carpet in a rustle of gray silk, pausing to press her hoop skirt to one side so she could negotiate the narrow doorway. As soon as the latch clicked shut, Aunt Penelope began to speak.

"That's a blessing," she said. "The girl should never have been up here in the first place. She has far too much imagination for this sort of business. I tried to tell her, but it's become apparent that I'm not really her guardian anymore, just a poor relation whose advice can be ignored. I'm happy that you, at least, had some influence over her."

Dr. Franklin rubbed his full white beard absentmindedly. "How did you ladies happen to be here before I arrived?"

"We had been invited for the evening, as a matter of fact, but I'm sure we'll have no dinner now. We were just arriving, when Reginald drove up in a carriage with his uncle and some men from the club to carry him upstairs. Of course we were obliged to stay and do anything we could. We're not far from being one family, you know."

"And you shall have your family dinner, never fear. I spoke to the servants about it. Starving the healthy is no help to the sick."

"I'm sure I couldn't eat a mouthful."

"Ah, but you must, dear lady, and you must see to it that the young people eat as well. Especially young Callender. A gentleman who prescribes himself such large doses of brandy must have a meal in him, too, or I'll end up with more than one patient in this house. You look like a sensible woman, with some experience of life, and I depend on you to take charge of things here, however much resistance you may meet."

He turned away without waiting for a reply and pulled a short wooden tube out of his bag.

"A stethoscope," said Aunt Penelope. "Very modern. Our own physician uses one as well. Much nicer for a lady than having someone press his ear against you, even if he is a medical man."

"That's as may be," said Dr. Franklin, "but its real value lies in its ability to amplify the sounds of the internal organs. If you will grant me a minute of silence, I shall endeavor to employ it."

She grew still as he pushed back the heavy bed curtains and pulled down the blankets that covered William Callender. Leaning over, Dr. Franklin put one end of the wooden tube to his ear and the other to his patient's chest. He shut his eyes in concentration. Aunt Penelope pushed her head forward as if she wished to listen too but could hear nothing except the crackling of the fire in the grate and the harsh, uneven sound of breathing from the bed.

At length Dr. Franklin straightened up and sighed, a sound so eloquent that even Aunt Penelope's eager curiosity at first prompted no question, at least not about the condition of the stricken man. She pursed her lips and shook her head.

"Are there no medicines?" she asked.

"Nothing I could administer without fear of choking him, I'm afraid. If I pour liquids down the throat of an unconscious man, I may kill him even faster than this seizure will. There should be more that we can do, and perhaps someday there will be. There's a man in Dublin, a Dr. Rynd, who has begun work on what he calls the subcutaneous introduction of fluids, but that's still in an experimental stage, if in fact it really works at all."

"Subcutaneous?"

"His work involves a device for injecting medicine directly through the skin and into the blood by means of some kind of hollow needle. But as I said, it's still only an idea. The only thing we can do for Mr. Callender's blood involves the work of my small friends here."

He picked up the glass jar that had fascinated Felicia, held it up to the candle's flame, and tapped it with one finger. "Time to go to work," he whispered to the shapes within. "Come, colleagues. Time to feed."

Aunt Penelope moved toward him. "Are they . . . " she began.

"*Hirudo medicinalis*," he replied.

"I beg your pardon?"

"Latin, my dear lady. A fancy name for the common leech."

He twisted off the top of the jar, placed it on the nightstand, and reached for a small, delicate pair of tongs. These he inserted carefully into the water, moving them about like a boy bobbing for apples until he had a firm but safe grasp on one of his wriggling helpers. He had no wish to injure one of these valuable assistants, and even less desire to find one attached to his own hand. The tiny triple jaws of the slippery creature contained teeth as sharp as needles and almost as difficult to dislodge. A bite did not hurt; something in the saliva of the little beasts killed the pain of the wounds they made even as it contrived to keep the blood flowing when it might otherwise have clotted. They were remarkably efficient little bloodsuckers, and very useful in their way, but Dr. Franklin always felt a tremor of distaste at the thought of one burrowing into his own flesh. After all, he was not a patient.

He applied the leech to the prominent, throbbing vein on one side of the stricken man's forehead, pausing to make sure that it was feeding firmly. As he reached for another, he glanced up and saw Penelope Lamb hovering beside him, her mouth half open as she craned her neck toward the leech squirming wetly in the grip of the tongs.

"Perhaps you would prefer to go below and see to dinner?" suggested Dr. Franklin.

"In a moment," whispered Aunt Penelope, shivering as she stared.

Dr. Franklin placed the second leech upon his patient's skin.

* * *

Black six on red seven.

Half slumped over his uncle William's desk, Reginald Callender took another gulp from his snifter of brandy as he surveyed the cards spread out before him. This was his fourth game of patience since he had helped to bring the stricken man back home, and so far none of his contests with the pasteboards had been successful. Yet he felt, for a reason he could never have explained, that it was important for him to defeat these inanimate objects, that somehow to win this contest against chance would be to win something else as well. He would not allow himself to think what that might be.

Red queen on black king.

Reginald Callender poured himself another large dose of brandy. He was quite deliberately embarked on a campaign to render himself insensible.

Surely, he told himself, he did not wish his uncle dead. Hadn't he called for help at once? Wasn't he so upset by the sight of him, feeble, crippled, unutterably mortal, that he was driven to drown the image in a sea of brandy?

Of course, the old boy was bound to die sooner or later. After all, everybody died. That's life, he thought, laughing dryly, almost immediately ashamed of the small sound.

Red five on black six.

He had always understood that his uncle would die someday and that on that sad occasion a fortune would pass into his hands. That was no more than common knowledge. And common sense. Even Uncle William would have acknowledged as much. There was nothing wrong in any of this; it was the order of things in an orderly world.

Since all of this was undeniably true, why did Reginald Callender feel consumed by guilt? He turned over another card, but it was of no use to him. He swallowed brandy. He listened to the ticking of the clock and watched a drop of molten wax slide over a silver candlestick.

He was afraid that he was waiting for a man's life to end.

He remembered himself as a boy, and he remembered the uncle William who had always been there with sweets, tin soldiers, and ready pocket money. The old fellow (he had seemed old even then) had offered the growing lad his first taste of brandy, and had even steered him toward his first wench when the time was right. He had been all but a father, and far more indulgent than many of those. Reginald Callender felt tears welling up in his eyes, as if he were already in mourning, but through his blurry vision he saw the glitter of gold.

Jack of spades on the queen of hearts.

The game was going well. He might win. The idea was not an unalloyed pleasure. How would he feel if he disposed of the last card and heard at once that the man upstairs had given up the ghost? Would he be responsible? What was he playing for? He was the victim of a childish bout of superstition, an irrational conviction that what he did with the cards would somehow affect the course of his uncle's illness. The idea was senseless, of course, but at least it was proof that he was succeeding in his principal objective. He was getting drunk. Soon he would be past caring what he did or what it meant.

He had just turned over the next card when he heard a tapping on the door, a sound so faint he might almost have imagined it.

He did not wish to look at the card he had just exposed. Instead, he glanced around at the walls, at the shelves of beautifully bound books that he had never read. He doubted if his uncle had read them either, and felt a cold certainty that neither of them ever would.

The gentle rapping came again, and with it a voice that was gentler still.

"Reginald?"

It was Felicia, the woman who soon would be his wife. A wealthy wife, evidently. Then again, she was wealthy already. He looked at the card in his hand: the nine of spades. It seemed to mean nothing, and there was nowhere for him to use it.

"Come in, Felicia," he said after a long pause.

She slipped quietly into the room and took his hand in hers. He was obliged to put down the cards.

"What is it, Felicia?" He looked into her pale eyes, lighter than the sky, and tried to read a message there. Her expression had a touch of melancholy, but that was nothing new. "What has happened?"

"Nothing, my dearest. The doctor is with your uncle now. And I have come to stay with you."

"He's dying, isn't he?"

"We must pray that he is not."

"Of course." He reached for the bottle of brandy with his free hand, more conscious than he liked to be of the pull she exerted on his other side. He looked for a flicker of disapproval in her face but saw only sadness and sympathy.

"There is nothing for you to fear," she said, kneeling beside his chair in a gesture that had nothing artificial in it but left him embarrassed nonetheless. He should have risen when she came in. Now, since he had failed even to offer her a chair, he found her at his feet, clutching at his left hand while he held the brandy in his right. He rose, pulling Felicia with him.

"Death is only a passage," she continued. "A journey to another land."

He sighed and poured himself another drink. "What are you talking about, Felicia?"

"I am trying to tell you what I have tried to tell you before, but you will never listen. Do you think that because I am a woman it follows that I am also a fool?"

"I never thought you were a fool, least of all because you were a woman. But how can you dream of death that way, when you've seen it in my uncle's face? It's horrible!"

"That's all illusion, Reginald. The flesh must be abandoned if the spirit will be free. If only you could hear Mr. Newcastle . . ."

"Newcastle? I hear more than enough of him from you! Is it not enough that Uncle William lies near death, without you invoking the name of this charlatan who preys upon the weak and ignorant? After we are wed we shall hear no more of Mr. Newcastle and his damned spirits!"

He yanked his fingers away from hers, downed his drink, and sat again at the desk. He reached for the deck of cards.

"Reginald, please," his fiancée began. "I meant only to reassure you . . ."

He turned over another useless card. "Reassure me of what, eh? What is it that we're to pray for? That Uncle William should live, or that he should die?"

His voice was rising to a shout, suddenly silenced when the library door burst open. Dr. Franklin stood on the threshold. "Pardon me," he said. "Is everything all right?"

"Right as rain," cried Reginald Callender. "And how are things above?"

"I'm sorry to say, sir, that your uncle—"

"Dead, is he? Well, don't tell me. Tell Newcastle!"

Cards spattered from the young man's fingers as he collapsed, insensible, across the surface of the desk. Franklin caught up a silver candlestick as it was knocked aside.

"Sorry, miss. Now we'll have to attend to him as well. It's often the way. Still, he'll be quite well tomorrow, except for the headache. How about you, Miss Lamb? Are you feeling faint?"

"Thank you, no."

"That's a blessing. The women in this house seem stronger than the men. Not uncommon, really. Will you call for some servants to take him to bed?"

"At once," Felicia said.

"And may I offer my carriage, to see you and your good aunt safely home?"

"Thank you," replied Felicia, nodding gravely before she hurried from the room.

Dr. Franklin gazed down at the sodden figure sprawled before him, his bed a puddle of playing cards soaked in brandy.

"Poor devil," said the old man. "And to think that soon you'll be rich."

THREE

Black Plumes

The boy on the steps had been paid to look unhappy, and he was doing his best, but he found it hard to mourn for a corpse he had never known, especially when the old man's death was making him money. Still, a job was a job, and Syd had no desire to lose this one. He stifled a smirk and glanced across the black-draped door toward his partner, but the sight of the old fellow with his fancy dress and his watery eyes was more than Syd could bear. He knew he must look just as foolish himself, wearing a top hat festooned with black crepe and carrying a long wand draped with more of the same, yet he felt a laugh rising in his chest that he barely succeeded in changing into a cough before it reached his lips. The crepe rustled, and Syd's partner altered his expression for an instant from dignified melancholy to threatening wrath. Mr. Callender had paid Entwistle and Son a substantial sum for a proper funeral, and that meant that the mutes would remain mute.

Syd stiffened, hoping that the procession would arrive soon to relieve him of his post. His nose itched, and his left foot seemed to have gone numb. After a whole morning standing on duty in front of Callender's house, Syd was beginning to look at the long march to All Souls as a positive pleasure. It would at least mean a bit of exercise, and it would bring Syd closer to the time when he would finally be able to make a little profit out of the business. There was no pay in being apprenticed to an undertaker, even if it was Entwistle and Son. Just the son now, actually, thought Syd, and it didn't look as if he could expect to live much longer himself, except that he couldn't bear the thought of dying and letting anybody else bury him. Entwistle and Son was the best there was, and the hearse Syd saw turning the corner from Kensington High Street proved it.

Six matched black horses drew the hearse, their heads crowned with bobbing black plumes of dyed peacock feathers, their backs covered with hangings of black velvet. The low black hearse, its glass sides etched in floral patterns, bore the oaken coffin upon a bed of lilies, under a canopy of more swaying black plumes. The driver proceeded at a measured pace to accommodate the mutes who trudged with downcast eyes beside the slowly rolling gilt-edged wheels. Behind them came the first mourning coach, and then the second; when the procession drew up before the house, Syd was startled to see that there were no more. It seemed incredible that such an expensive funeral should have so few mourners; Syd could hardly believe that a man rich enough to afford Entwistle's best had so few friends.

The son himself stepped from the second coach, the crepe on his hat fluttering across his face in the brisk autumn breeze. Syd snapped to attention like the soldiers he had seen outside Buckingham Palace guarding the Queen, and stared straight ahead as the undertaker glided up the steps with the black cloth alternately masking and unmasking his pale and furrowed face. Syd had learned long ago not to fear the dead, but he still feared the man who tended them, and he did not look to the side when he heard the sound of the brass door knocker. Shuffling steps approached the door, and the latch clicked.

"Mr. Callender, please," said Mr. Entwistle. "Mr. Callender asks that you wait for him outside," came the reply. The door closed quietly.

Syd stood so rigidly that he began to tremble as Mr. Entwistle made his way stiffly down the steps and toward the second coach. Syd's feelings were a mixture of shock and delight; he saw that the expression on the face of his fellow mute was now genuinely grief-stricken. It was a revelation to discover a household too grand to receive Mr. Entwistle, and Syd was far too impressed to do anything but stare when the door opened again to let the funeral party out.

There was a fat butler, a young gentleman with sandy side-whiskers, and a little lady with gray hair, but what Syd noticed was the one who stood behind them in the shadows. Her skin was fair, her eyes were of the lightest blue, and her hair was a blond that was nearly white. There was next to no color in her, and she was as beautiful as a statue. All of them were dressed in black, and the little lady had the younger one by the arm.

"There's no need for you to come, Felicia," she said. "It's not the sort of thing a young lady ought to see."

"And yet you're going, Aunt Penelope."

"I'm no longer a young lady, and we can't send Mr. Callender off alone on such a sad errand."

"But surely my place is with Reginald, Aunt Penelope."

"You've done more than enough for him already, and if he loves you, he wouldn't dream of exposing you to such an ordeal. Besides, you're needed here to keep an eye on the servants, or there won't be much left of the feast by the time we return."

Neither the butler nor his master made any comment on this or anything else, but when the older woman said "I'll hear no more about it," the young gentleman took her arm and the butler closed the door behind them. Syd, whose only concern had been the pale angel who stayed behind, recollected himself and returned to his job, escorting Reginald Callender and the angel's aunt Penelope to the first mourning coach. One of the horses stirred despite its blinders as they passed; everything else was still but Aunt Penelope's tongue.

"A gray day is just as well for a funeral, I think. It's appropriately solemn, but not really unpleasant. The day we buried poor Felicia's parents, the rain was so heavy it was almost a storm, and the child was crying so much on top of it, I don't think I've ever been so wet in all my born days. I really think it affected her, too. She's always been so delicate. A sunny day's not right, either, though. I remember

51

burying a cousin when the day was so fine that it spoiled the whole occasion. It just wasn't fitting. No, I think a gray day is best."

She gestured decisively with her fan of black plumes and waited for Syd to open the carriage door.

"Uncle William chose the day, not I," said Reginald Callender as he helped Aunt Penelope up the step.

"Nonsense! If your uncle William had his choice, this day never would have come at all. He would much rather have spent his fortune than left it all to you, Mr. Callender. Not that you'll need it, with such a wealthy wife soon to be yours. It is a fine thing, though, is it not, to see two family fortunes joined along with their heirs?"

"No doubt," replied Callender as the door shut behind them, and he took his seat beside his fiancée's aunt. His head throbbed already and he realized that burying his uncle would be more of an ordeal than whatever grief he felt would warrant. Last night he had taken too much whiskey, to calm his nerves and muffle his tactless conviction that he was, in his hour of bereavement, the luckiest man alive. What more could a man wish for but riches and a beautiful wife, except to be free of the headache and a chattering woman who seemed to dote on death?

"It's a tragedy, the funeral party being so small, don't you think? Of course, everything has been done in the very height of fashion, but it seems a shame that nobody's here to enjoy it."

"My uncle survived all his partners by some years, and I am his last living relative, as you know. The last of the Callenders. There is simply no one left to mourn him."

"And Felicia looked so lovely in that black silk! She can't keep wearing it, you know; she's not really in mourning, but it was so dear that it certainly should be seen. I took her to Jay's in Regent Street, you know. They make a specialty of mourning, and they furnished both of us for your uncle's funeral."

"Very handsomely, to be sure," murmured Callender, laying a hand beside his head in a gesture that he hoped would suggest intelligent interest while still providing him with the opportunity to massage an aching temple. The motion of the coach was beginning to make him slightly sick.

"Of course, I've had dresses from Jay's before; so many of one's friends and family seem to die as the years pass. I think the widow's weeds are most attractive, but a woman can't be a widow before she's a wife, can she?"

Callender might have answered, but Aunt

Penelope had turned from him to gaze out of the coach at the streets of London. "I see you have chosen to travel by way of the park," she said. "Very wise, I'm sure. I thought you might have chosen the shorter route instead, where we should hardly have been seen at all."

"It was my uncle's wish," said Callender. "He left instructions for his funeral with his solicitor, Mr. Frobisher."

"What a clever man! I never thought of such a thing, but I must certainly make plans for my own passing at the first possible moment. Of course, I have no fortune to compensate my heirs for the expense. . . ."

"I am sure that Felicia will be happy to accommodate you," sighed Callender.

"Do you think so? Yes, I suppose she will. Such a generous girl, and such a spiritual nature. Her thoughts are always with the angels."

Callender wished fervently that Aunt Penelope could be with the angels, too. He closed his eyes and thought of Felicia. Just a moment's peace would be enough to bring him sleep.

"Then Kensal Green was your uncle's choice as well?"

"I beg your pardon?" said Callender, pulling himself back to consciousness.

"Kensal Green, I said. All Souls Cemetery. It's certainly where I would choose to rest in peace. I visit there sometimes, and I still think it's the loveliest cemetery in London, even when compared with those that have opened since. The first of anything is often the best, don't you think? And, of course, anything would be better than one of the old church-yards. You must have heard the stories about the pestilence bred in those awful places, and about the way the skeletons were dug up and stored in sheds to make way for more graves? It's enough to make a body shudder."

Callender looked to see if she was shudder-ing, and almost thought he saw her waving at a passerby. Although thoroughly dismayed by her enjoyment of the proceedings, he decided to resign himself to her display. He had little choice in any case, and a day of pleasure for his beloved's maiden aunt was a small enough additional tax on the life of happiness that lay before him. He settled back in his seat as the coach rolled on.

Felicia Lamb closed her book and sat for a moment staring into space. Critics had savaged the novel and its unknown author, Ellis Bell, and Felicia admitted to herself that she had sometimes been dismayed by the savagery of its setting and the brutishness of its characters. Yet something in the story had compelled her interest: the idea of an immortal love that transcended even death. Such a passion both fascinated and frightened her; half of her longed for something like it, but destiny had decided to provide her with a much more practical match. Reginald Callender had his virtues, as her Aunt Penelope was frequently at pains to point out, but she could hardly imagine anyone accusing him of a supernatural longing. Perhaps it was just as well, Felicia thought. She knew that she was inclined toward morbidity as certainly as was her father's sister, so it was possible that her fiancé had been sent to help her keep her feet firmly planted on the ground. They were equals in rank and fortune; the marriage made sense.

She sighed and placed the last volume of *Wuthering Heights* on the highly polished surface of the table in the center of the drawing room. What light from the afternoon sky that managed to press through the heavy curtains was weak and dismal; the pendulum of the clock in the corner seemed to push the hours on toward darkness. Surely it was late enough for Reginald and Aunt Penelope to have returned. Against her will Felicia pictured a terrible accident that might at one blow deprive her of the only two people she could consider family. She realized it was a foolish fancy, yet she had lost both her parents at once a dozen years ago and knew all too well that such things were possible. She had more faith in the next world than she had in her chances for happiness in this.

She gazed up at the portrait of Reginald's uncle William that hung magisterially over the mantel, and she wondered where he was now. The round, ruddy face and the thick body were, of course, in a coffin under six feet of earth, but where was William Callender himself? And where were her mother and father? The spirits of the dead haunted her without ever appearing as phantoms; perhaps she would have been less troubled if they had. She longed for Reginald to return and pull her away from such brooding, even though she always half resented him when he did. Was she right to marry him, or anyone at all?

"Shall I light the fire, miss?"

A ghost would have startled her less than did the voice, but she realized in an instant that it was only the butler. And while she doubted that flames could eliminate the chill she felt within her, a cheery fire would be welcome to anyone returning from a long funeral on a raw autumn day.

"Thank you, Booth. I think Mr. Callender would appreciate it." She heard his knees creak as he bent before the picture of his late master, and she felt a twinge of regret that she had not tended to the matter herself; it would have been much easier for her than it was for the old man. Her guilt propelled her from the room to supervise the preparations for the funeral feast, but she was not really needed for that, either.

"Is everything ready, Alice?" she asked the pretty, dark-haired maid. The girl, whose black uniform had lost its white ruffles to the dignity of the day, gave Felicia a curtsy and a small smile.

"Oh, yes, miss, thank you. Mr. Entwistle's people took care of everything themselves, and it's very nice, I'm sure."

The sideboard was covered with food: a ham, a roast of beef, bread, pies, cakes, and bottles of sherry and port. There was enough to feed dozens of people, though only three were to be served.

"So much?" asked Felicia, without stopping to consider the propriety of conversing with the servants on matters of form.

"Oh, yes, miss. I asked them if there might be some mistake, but the gentleman assured me it was all called for in Mr. Callender's will. May I serve you something, miss?"

"Thank you, no," answered Felicia, who

had never felt less hungry in her life. "I'll wait for the others, Alice. Do I hear them coming in now?"

"I'll go see, miss," the maid said as she scurried off.

A moment later Felicia was joined by her aunt Penelope, her eyes bright beneath her black bonnet as she surveyed the lavish meal spread out before her. "Well," she said, "this is very handsomely done, Felicia. And so it should be, I say. Weddings and funerals are important occasions. Will you pour me a glass of sherry, dear? Just a small one."

Aunt Penelope popped a small cake into her mouth as Reginald Callender strode into the room and reached for the bottle of port. He filled a glass and swallowed it at once.

"A lovely funeral, Mr. Callender," said Aunt Penelope. "And the mausoleum was very splendid indeed. Did your uncle make provisions for you to join him there when you are called?"

Callender made no reply except to pour himself another drink. He collected himself enough to offer a glass to Felicia, but she refused it and seated herself on a small straight-backed chair in a corner.

"I don't think I approve of closed coffins, however," said Aunt Penelope.

Callender's face turned suddenly hard. "Surely you saw enough of my uncle when he was lying in state, didn't you?"

"Oh, to be sure, Mr. Callender. I meant no criticism. Sometimes, I suppose, the last look may be too painful to endure. Would you be kind enough to slice me some of that ham? Thank you. And how have you spent the day, Felicia?"

"In thinking of those who have gone before us, Aunt."

"Oh? And what were your conclusions, dear?"

"Only that there is much to know, and that we know very little of it," said Felicia.

"Perhaps you will be wiser tomorrow evening, after our visit to Mr. Newcastle."

Felicia's eyes widened, and she glanced anxiously back and forth between her aunt and her fiancé.

"Newcastle? And who, pray tell, is Mr. Newcastle, that you should visit him at night?" demanded Callender, brandishing the carving knife as he passed a plate of ham to Aunt Penelope.

"Why, the spirit medium, of course," she said as she took the plate. "We passed his house on the way to Kensal Green."

Felicia sank back farther into her corner under Callender's accusing stare. "I know too well who he is!" Callender roared as he turned back to Aunt Penelope. "Is this some of your nonsense?"

"It is my own idea, Reginald," Felicia said quietly.

"I positively forbid it."

"You will forbid me nothing before I become your wife. You know how I long to know what lies beyond this life. Why should you want to deny me?"

"Because it's all fraud and nonsense and superstition. How can an intelligent girl like you believe in such antiquated fancies in this day and age? This is 1847, and we are in an age of progress, when such things should be cast aside once and for all."

"We progress in many things, Reginald; and why should not the knowledge of what lies beyond the veil be one of them? You must have heard of what Mr. David Home has achieved, and I believe that Mr. Newcastle's gifts are even more remarkable. I am certain that there are persons with the ability to see things that are invisible to us."

"What they see that's invisible to you is that you are a gullible woman with too much money. What's dead is dead, Felicia, and best forgotten."

She rose from her chair and clasped her hands together earnestly. "But the dead do live on, Reginald. How can you doubt it? Aren't you a Christian?"

Callender hacked viciously at the ham. "Yes, I'm a Christian. Church of England every Sunday, and money in the plate. But what do you think the Reverend Mr. Fisher would say if he knew you were raising spooks? And what do you really know about this fellow Newcastle? He might be a lunatic. It isn't safe, and I ask you again to forget this folly."

"I have promised to act as my niece's chaperone," volunteered Aunt Penelope as she helped herself to more sherry. "And in exchange she has agreed to accompany me to the Dead Room at Madame Tussaud's. Neither of us is quite brave enough to indulge her fancy alone, but we do intend to have our curiosity satisfied, Mr. Callender."

"What? The place *Punch* calls the Chamber of Horrors? That's a fine place for a sensitive girl, I must say, but at least I suppose it's harmless. This master of goblins is quite another matter. He's either a charlatan or a madman, and the fact that you are two helpless females instead of one does nothing to reassure me. I'll wager he wants more than a few shillings for admission, eh?"

Aunt Penelope moved to her niece's side and put a hand on her shoulder, which Felicia took gratefully.

"We shall not be dissuaded," said Aunt Penelope.

Callender smiled ruefully. "Then I suppose I must accompany you," he said.

"Oh, Reginald, will you?" Felicia asked eagerly. "Please come with us. I hope to speak with my mother and father again, and perhaps Mr. Newcastle will let you commune with your uncle William."

"I trust my uncle William is happy where he is, Felicia, and I would not wish to drag him down again to the clay, even if I believed I could. Let him rest in peace, I say."

He put his arms around Felicia and led her across the room to a love seat as far removed as possible from the food that the dead man had ordered. "Can you not forget the dead?" he asked her. "We are among the living now, and whatever questions we have to ask of our forebears will be answered in due time. Until then it is our duty to live our lives as best we can. Will you live for me instead of these idle dreams?"

Felicia's fingers stroked his face, but her eyes remained distant. "How can we know what we should do," she demanded, "when we do not know what lies ahead of us? How much pleasure can we take here, when we know it is only a school for the lessons we shall learn?"

63

"We may have been born to die," said Callender, "but that is only part of it. The pleasures offered to us here are not our enemies. We are young and wealthy, Felicia. We are blessed. Let us not spurn fate's favors."

"He's right, you know," said Aunt Penelope as she cut into a pie. "We shall be quit of this world soon enough without denying it. But still, Mr. Callender, we shall make our visits."

"And if you must," he said, "I shall be with you."

He might have said more, but the butler interrupted him.

"Yes, Booth?" he murmured as the old man bent down to whisper into his ear. Callender rose, bowed to the ladies, and hurried out into the hall.

There in the twilight stood the gaunt form of Mr. Entwistle. "I know how these things are, sir," he said, "and I would not wish to keep you waiting." He handed Callender a few small objects tied in a handkerchief. "His rings, his pins, and his watch," he said.

Callender cringed but thanked the undertaker nonetheless.

"I understand entirely," said Mr. Entwistle. "It is not all uncommon for young gentlemen to experience a temporary embarrassment while waiting for the reading of the will. You may be sure that your uncle's estate will compensate us for our trouble." He bowed and slithered back into the gathering darkness.

Reginald Callender stood with his uncle's jewelry in his hand, and a wave of disgust poured over him. While Felicia worried about souls, he was forced to concern himself with the problem of raising enough money to keep the household in order. It was hardly gentlemanly behavior; it was almost like robbing the dead. Still, his uncle's adornments had been visible in the open coffin when he had lain in state. Now they had been rescued from the grave. Supported since childhood by the investments of his mother's brother, Callender truly had no idea of how to support himself except to sell what came to hand. It was only a temporary aberration, he told himself; soon the estate would make him rich.

Still, he was angry with himself, and more angry with Felicia for concerning herself with spirits when he was so desperate for material comfort. He saw the maid hurrying across the hallway and called out to her.

"Alice," he said, "come here for a moment."

The girl came slowly toward him.

"Are you happy with your position here?"

"Oh, yes, sir," said Alice.

"And were you happy with my uncle?"

Alice blushed and nodded.

"Then we shall continue the same arrangement now that I am master."

"Just as you say, sir," said Alice.

"Very well. My visitors will be leaving soon. I shall expect you later this evening, Alice. Everything will be as it was before. Come at ten. And bring my uncle's riding crop."

FOUR

The Resurrection Men

The boy with the crowbar strapped to his leg ordered another pint of beer. He rarely drank the stuff because it cost too much and he had no head for it anyway, but tonight he felt as jumpy as a cat, and was certain of enough money to buy a whole barrel if he liked. And anyway, he told himself, it would be Syd's fault if he got drunk. They had agreed to meet an hour ago in this pub, The World Turned Upside Down, and since Syd was so late, it had become necessary to keep buying beer. He could hardly expect to stay indoors without spending money, and even at that there had been a few jokes about his age, but Henry Donahue was unconcerned. He was fifteen, after all, old enough to drink all he could hold, and old enough to rob a grave. Still, he wished Syd would hurry.

Henry had picked the place himself, even though he had never been inside before, partly for its proximity to Kensal Green and partly because he had always liked its sign. Whether the globe on it was really upside down he could not have said, but something in the idea appealed to him. And things were quiet enough inside, which he supposed was good, though he would have preferred enough of a crowd to make him feel a bit less conspicuous. He was looking around the dim room, convinced that all the other patrons were watching him, when he saw the door open and Syd's sharp, pimply face peer in. Henry gulped down the last of his drink and walked briskly toward the door. Syd was halfway in, but Henry pushed him out again.

"Let me come in for a minute, will you?" protested Syd.

"You're late enough without dawdling here any longer, don't you think?"

"I know, I know, but I'm cold enough already, aren't I? Is it my fault if I couldn't get away?"

"It'll be your fault if we're any later, Syd. I can't be out all night, you know."

"You smell like you already have been,

68

mate. A fine thing, drinking on the job. You won't be much good for picking locks now, will you?"

Henry grabbed Syd's arm to quiet him. A lamplighter was shuffling down the empty street toward them, the yellow fog of London dimming the light of the small hand-lamp he carried. The two boys leaned against the building with feigned unconcern, Henry gazing at the sign while Syd read the words guaranteeing the availability of Courage and Company's Entire, and wondered how much of it Henry had consumed. The old man climbed up his short ladder, turned the gas cock, applied his lamp, and scrambled down again, leaving the entrance to the public house only a little brighter than it had been before. The boys waited till his footsteps had died away.

"You were really scared of him, weren't you?" sneered Syd. "Maybe you should run home now and forget all this, Henry."

"I'm not scared of anything. But there's no point in letting anyone know what we're up to, is there? Burke and Hare were hanged, weren't they?"

"They were murderers, you dunce, and we're not even stealing bodies. There's no market for 'em anymore, is there? All we're doing is relieving the old gent of some jewelry that he'll never miss. It would be a crime to let it rot with him, wouldn't it?"

"Not a crime you can be charged with," Henry said.

"Well, if you don't want the money, mate, you run along."

But Henry was already walking toward the cemetery, pulling his cap down over his shaggy red hair and turning his collar up against the cold and the eyes of passersby.

"You're sure he's got all that stuff on him, are you, Syd?"

"I saw it, didn't I? There's not much else to do when you work for an undertaker but look at the bodies. Just like there's not much for an apprentice locksmith to do but learn how to open things. I've just been waiting to meet a partner like you, Henry. We're in business now, you know, and we have splendid prospects."

The closer they got to Kensal Green, the more unhappy Henry was. The houses were fewer, the lights were farther apart, and the fog filled the empty spaces. Henry began to feel as if he were lost somewhere out in the countryside and would happily have turned back at once except for a certain reluctance to disgrace himself in front of Syd: It was easier to face corpses or even the police than to admit to a boy a year older than himself that he wanted nothing more of life than to be back in a garret.

Henry watched his feet pass over the damp cobblestones; they were almost all he could see. The dark was bad enough, but the fog was worse. "We'll never find it," Henry said.

"What do you mean, we'll never find it? We're here!"

Henry looked up and saw something like a temple looming through the mist. There were columns and walls and fences, and it looked to him less like a churchyard than like the Bank of England. The gigantic gates were clearly locked, and he could perceive nothing behind them but another wall of impenetrable fog.

"I don't want to open those gates," he said. "Someone might come along."

"Don't worry," Syd insisted. "We'll just climb the wall."

"What's the use?" asked Henry, turning away. "We can't find anything in there. The fog."

"I know where it is, don't I? How many times have I been here, eh? It's my job. Just give me a leg up. Come on, over here."

Henry almost ran away, but instead, he hurried toward the sound of Syd's voice. Finding the other boy, he was relieved to touch someone else, even if it was his partner in a crime that he would have willingly abandoned. At least he was not alone. He squatted close to the ground, where the air was a little clearer, and made his hands into a cradle for Syd's foot.

Syd scrambled up, and Henry thought for an instant that he had broken a wrist. He grunted, then lost Syd in the fog. "Where are you? Are you up?" A hand dropped down to him.

"Here. Grab it. Come on. Get off the street!"

Henry seized Syd's wrist and felt himself hauled up against the wall, scraping and squirming until he reached the top. "You're up?" said Syd. "Then drop down." Suddenly Henry was alone again.

He looked into the opaque night, shivered at the thought of an observer, and fell into darkness. He landed on Syd, and both of them tumbled on the wet grass of All Souls Cemetery.

"That's fine. Kill us both."

"Are we in? Where are we, Syd?"

"Kensal Green, my boy. We're in. Follow me."

"Wait a minute, Syd! Where are you? You can't know where we're going."

"I tell you I know this place like I know my mother, even if I haven't seen her for years."

"Give us your hand, then, will you? I'm lost."

"Take hold, then. You'll hold a prettier hand than this one, once we're done."

Henry hung on to Syd, wandering through a sea of fog that might have been heaven or hell. From time to time a monument loomed up, a spire or an angel or a slab. Some of them were huge. Syd dragged him through the clouds. It was so cold that his nose began to run, and all at once he was hungry. "We'll never find it, Syd. Let's go home."

"No? We'll never find it?"

Something sat in the fog. Henry blinked twice. "It's big enough," he said.

"The lock is small."

A gray box squatted in the yellow fog. A stone box, its roof pointed, with pillars beside the door. Two figures made of marble stood on either side of the door; they looked to Henry like women in nightshirts. He couldn't see much, but what he saw was enough.

Syd knocked on the door while Henry shuddered. "Mr. Callender's residence?"

"Don't do that, Syd."

"No? Think he'll wake up, do you? Don't worry, I threw his guts away myself. If he did rise up, he'd fall right over."

"That's not funny."

"Don't laugh, then. Just open the door."

"I can't."

"You haven't even tried yet. You're terrified, that's what's wrong with you."

"I can't even see, can I? How do you expect me to work?"

"I got a bunch of lucifers, and I told you what the lock is like. Just work. The sooner you start, the sooner we'll be out of here."

Syd lit a match, and the way it colored his eyes was enough to send Henry toward the lock. He reached into his pocket and produced several instruments.

"I'd love to know how to work those."

"I'll teach you. Then you can do this by yourself."

"Don't be like that. Just a few more minutes, and we'll be rich men, Henry. You take care of the lock, and I'll take care of the body, all right?"

"Splendid," muttered Henry, his stiff fingers fumbling. He heard something snap, then wished he hadn't. Syd pushed him toward the metal door, and it fell away before them into hideous blackness. Henry twitched and looked toward the sky, but all he saw was the name "Callender" carved in the marble over his head. He lost his balance and sprawled against a wet wall as Syd shoved him into the house of the dead. The stink of dying flowers turned his stomach. He sat down in a corner and watched Syd strike another match and light a candle with it. The light flickered around stone walls like slabs. Henry looked outside and glimpsed a shadow. "There's something out there, Syd."

"Ghosts."

"Don't be smart; I saw a dog."

"Then shut the door and he won't see us."

"Too late for that," Henry said, but he pushed the iron door back.

Immediately he felt trapped. He hurriedly caught the edge of the door before it could swing shut, pulled the crowbar out from under the leg of his ragged trousers, and braced it against the jamb. The opening allayed his fear slightly, even when he saw wisps of fog drift through it, but Syd was not pleased with his handiwork.

"What do you think you're doing with that, then? Have you been walking stiff-legged all night so we could have a doorstop? I need that crowbar! Give it here."

Henry handed it over reluctantly, unhappy to be farther from the exit and closer to the sinister oblong of stone that brooded in the center of the small, dark room. Syd stuck the candle to the floor with its drippings, then turned to the sarcophagus and began to pry off its lid. Henry backed away at the hideous sound of scraping, grating stone and put one foot outside the tomb, relieved to find that they were not imprisoned by some uncanny force. Syd pushed and grunted against the ponderous weight while Henry prayed that he would fail to move it.

"You could help," gasped Syd.

"A bargain's a bargain. The lock was my job. The body's yours."

"It's only another box in there. It won't hurt you."

"I know it won't, since I'm not going near it."

"All right, then!" Syd threw himself furiously on the bar, and the stone slab tilted ominously. For an instant he hung counterbalanced in the air; then the lid screeched and fell to the floor with a crash that sounded to Henry like the end of the world. At the same instant Syd dropped on the other side and snuffed out the candle. The echoing tomb was black.

"Oh, my God," whispered Henry.

"He's not likely to be much help to you when you're on a job like this one, is he, mate?"

Something shuffled in the dark, and another of Syd's matches burst into flame, making his face as red as a painted devil's, but no less reassuring to Henry for that. He was amazed to discover that he had not run away, then realized that he had been too startled to move. Syd lit the broken candle and handed it to him. "Hold this," he said.

"I don't want to look."

"Of course you do. I'll bet that's half of why you came."

Henry didn't answer, but neither did he turn away when Syd approached the oaken coffin in its bed of stone. The candle flame shimmered in his shaking hand, and he knew without a doubt that when the coffin opened, a hideously moldering corpse would rise from its depths and drag them straight to hell. He thought he heard a dog howl somewhere outside. He closed his eyes. Wood creaked, and then he heard Syd groan. The groan rose into a wail.

"We've been robbed!"

"What?" Henry opened his eyes, and for an instant saw nothing but Syd's furious red face.

"Look for yourself! It must have been old Entwistle, the grasping, bloody bastard. He's taken it all. The rings, the watch, the stickpin, too. There's nothing here but the damn body!"

Unwilling to believe his ears, Henry moved forward with the light until he could see into the coffin. He swiftly checked the pale fingers and the black cravat. Nothing gleamed on them. He began to curse, then realized that he was staring into the face of a dead man.

It was not as bad as he had imagined. Just a plump old boy with rosy cheeks, really nothing to be afraid of; he looked as if he were taking a nap. It was only when Henry's nostrils caught the mingled odors of flowers, chemicals, and death that his stomach began to heave.

The iron door behind him crashed open.

Henry screamed, dropped the candle, and spun toward the sound. Silhouetted against the foggy night stood the gigantic figure of a man, his outstretched arms barring the way out of the tomb. Henry's mind went blank, his fanciful fear of the corpse forgotten in the sudden and very real conviction that he was doomed. The blood drained out of his face as he saw himself on the gallows, and he could hold on to only one idea: I'm caught, I'm caught, I'm caught. He hardly heard the low, calm voice of the figure at the door.

"Have you found what you seek?"

Henry was amazed to hear Syd's brassy answer.

"Nah, there's nothing here. Somebody's stripped him bare."

Another match flared. Syd's hand was steady, his expression insolent. "Bring that candle over here, will you, Henry?"

Henry was startled into action, almost believing that Syd's boldness might somehow set them free. Not even the second flame showed much of the dark intruder's face as he spoke again.

"These dead are mine."

"And welcome to 'em," answered Syd, moving toward the doorway with the crowbar held behind his back. Henry followed him like a somnambulist, but stopped dead when he saw the tall man's face. The skin was pale under long, stringy black hair; the lips were hidden by a drooping black mustache; the eyes seemed no more than dark hollows, the left bisected by a scar that ran from brow to chin. The countenance was so expressionless that it might have been a mask.

"That's not the caretaker," Henry heard himself saying, "it's that spirit reader from across the way."

"That's torn it," said Syd, and he swung for the man's head with the crowbar. The blow never landed. Henry stood frozen and watched a long white hand shoot out to grasp Syd's wrist while another attached itself to his face, the fingers scrabbling like a pale spider. The man opened his arms in a gesture that seemed almost hospitable, and Syd's hand came off at the wrist in a shower of blood while the flesh of his face was ripped from the bones.

Henry dropped the candle again and dove for the darkness where the door had been.

He tumbled to the ground in a blind panic and crawled through the yellow fog. He thought about God. He ran.

A tree stopped him. It bloodied his nose and broke two fingers, but he got up and ran again.

A low tombstone caught him just below the kneecap. He rolled in the wet grass and whimpered. Then he arose and limped away.

He couldn't see where he was going, but he didn't stop until the agony of his broken leg compelled him to. He rested under a marble angel and waited for death to come.

It came on black wings.

FIVE

The Spiritualist

The house near the cemetery where he had buried his uncle William was so nondescript that Reginald Callender scarcely remembered having passed it twice before. He was almost disappointed. He had expected either something gaudy or else picturesquely dilapidated and sinister, but Mr. Sebastian Newcastle's dwelling was an unpretentious house of good English brick, perhaps fifty years old. The tall cypresses surrounding it had a slightly funereal air, but that was all. Every window was dark but one, which glowed faintly through the fog.

Callender had accompanied Felicia and her aunt Penelope despite his misgivings; he was not a man to tolerate argument from a woman, especially one he expected to have as his bride, and he was deeply suspicious of Felicia's interest in this spirit medium, who was certainly a charlatan and probably a criminal who preyed on the sentiments of bereaved ladies. Still, the fact that the man he already thought of as his enemy was so unpretentious in his tastes gave Callender pause. Subtlety always irritated him.

He helped Aunt Penelope out of the coach, and then Felicia, listening with approval when she told the driver to wait. Soon he would be giving orders to her servants himself, but until his uncle's estate could be settled, he had so little cash on hand that he had been obliged to dismiss his own coachman; although he could hardly get along without the household servants, especially Alice. She would have to go soon enough, he told himself, but a glance at Felicia told him that the sacrifice would be worthwhile. Sometimes he wondered why it was necessary to wed a lady in order to bed her, but that was the way of the world, and meanwhile there were willing wenches in it.

A shapeless shadow flitted across the window as they approached the house, one of the ladies on each of his arms, and the look of it somehow sickened him, but they did not seem to have noticed. He opened his mouth to renew his arguments about the foolish recklessness of the business they were embarked upon, then thought better of it. He had already decided to show them the truth. The old woman was simply a sensation seeker and would be just as happy to discover that the spiritualist was a fraud, but Felicia was something of a fanatic on the subject, and that would never do for Reginald Callender's wife. Still, this night's work should settle that, and another night's work, after the wedding, would provide her with a new interest in life. Determined to take matters in his own hands, Callender rapped on the door with a gloved fist.

While he waited impatiently, Felicia reached past him and pulled on a narrow, rattling chain that he had never noticed. "The bell," she explained. "He may not hear you knocking from upstairs."

"No lights upstairs," said Callender. "Besides, I saw someone move down here, unless it was one of his confederates."

"Mr. Newcastle has no need of confederates, nor has he any need of light."

Aunt Penelope, thrilled into temporary silence by her approach to the land that lies beyond death, gave a little squeal when the door opened abruptly.

A tall man stood on the threshold, a silver candlestick held in his hand, a single flame illuminating a lean, pale face that was shadowed by black hair and a long mustache. Callender was startled for a moment by the scar, then dismissed it as an effective theatrical touch and spent most of the next few minutes trying to decide if it was real. The man, who was quite clearly Newcastle rather than a servant, stepped back silently and ushered them into an empty hall, a dusty carpet of no determinable pattern on the floor.

At the end of the hallway was a double door, and beyond that a room that seemed unnaturally dark even after their host had brightened it with his lone candle. Callender saw that both the floor and the ceiling had been painted black, and that black velvet draperies completely covered the walls. A small round table in the room's center was surrounded by four high-backed wooden chairs; all of the furniture appeared to have been made of ebony. The medium set his candlestick in the middle of the table and stood quietly, waiting for his visitors to follow him into the gloomy chamber. His clothing was as black as Callender's mourning, so that only his white face and hands were distinctly visible, apparently floating disembodied in the air. When the ladies entered with their dark cloaks and bonnets, the effect was much the same, and Callender had no reason to believe that he looked any different. The illusion was disconcerting.

The two women sat down across from each other, but Reginald Callender remained on his feet, squinting into the shadows where Sebastian Newcastle's eyes were hidden. He expected the spiritualist to flinch before his penetrating stare, but the fellow was imperturbable, and ultimately it was Callender who turned away in what he told himself was pure disdain. A mounting sense of irritation caused him to break the long silence at last.

"Well! Bring on your spooks, sir, or must we pay you for them first?"

"Reginald!" Felicia's voice was harsher than he had ever heard it, and before he knew what had happened, he was seated beside her, feeling very much like a chastened schoolboy and wondering for the first time if married life might be something less than pleasant. Aunt Penelope suppressed a nervous giggle. Callender had a deep desire to lash out at someone but had difficulty deciding who it should be. Sebastian Newcastle sat down across the table from him.

"There will be no charge for your visit, Mr. Callender, since I do not expect you to enjoy it."

"I don't know; I've always enjoyed conjuring tricks, but you won't find me as easy to fool as some of your visitors."

"Miss Lamb and her aunt are hardly fools,

Mr. Callender, even if they do seek to be still wiser than they are. And have you never wondered what waits beyond the grave?"

"We have churches to tell us that, and not for money."

"Your churches are far richer than I am, and likely to remain so."

"Well, Mr. Newcastle, you'll have a chance to change that tonight. Here's ten guineas." Callender reached into his waistcoat pocket and placed the money on the table. He could ill afford to lose it. "If I see anything here that I cannot explain, that belongs to you." He pointed emphatically to the cash and noticed to his amazement that it was gone. "By God!" he said. "These are very materialistic spirits, sir."

"You will find that they have returned the money to your pocket, Mr. Callender."

Callender felt for the money and almost forgot himself enough to curse.

"Is it there?" asked Aunt Penelope.

"I think Reginald's face answers that question," observed Felicia coldly. "Really, Reginald, we have not come here to insult our host, but to learn from him. Do be quiet, if only to please me. Mr. Newcastle has promised to summon my parents tonight."

"Your parents were killed in a railway accident twelve years ago, Felicia, and if your

father had not been one of the chief stockholders in that railway, this man would have
no interest in him or in you."

"He will certainly have no interest if you
will not give him the peace he needs to pierce
the veil."

Callender reminded himself again that he
had determined to hold his tongue and realized ruefully that he should have done so.
Even Aunt Penelope had said almost nothing.

"Silence is an aid to concentration," Newcastle said evenly.

Callender nodded almost imperceptibly
and was delighted to find himself rewarded at
once when Felicia took his hand. He was
more than a little startled, though, when Aunt
Penelope did the same. He then surmised that
this was common behavior at a séance. Still, it
took all his willpower to refrain from comment when he saw his fiancée's delicate fingers in the pale clutch of the man with the
dark eyes.

The four of them sat quietly in the black
room, Callender never taking his eyes from
the medium, who gradually sank back in his
chair and allowed his head to slump forward.
He looked like an old man dozing after a
heavy dinner, reminding Callender of his uncle William. After a few minutes the atmosphere grew chilly, and Callender was almost

convinced that he felt a damp breeze waft past him, although he could see no way it could have come into the room. It was enough to make him look around uncomfortably, taking his eyes off the medium just long enough for something strange to happen.

For a moment Callender thought the man might be on fire. Vague tendrils of smoke seemed to be rising from his head, but they looked more like mist than smoke, and they wove patterns in the air that did not seem natural. Callender turned to his right and left, but the two women holding his hands were not dismayed and seemed to be regarding the display with intelligent approval. The medium groaned; his head was almost hidden by shifting fingers of mist. He seemed to be dissolving into the darkness. Callender started involuntarily and had half risen from his chair, when a blast of frigid wind roared at him from across the table. The candle flame went out.

He felt Felicia's grip on his fingers increase till it was almost painful, and a certain unexpected weakness in his knees compelled him to sink down into his seat again. Nothing was visible except the writhing cloud of mist, which seemed to glow with its own faint luminescence. He tried to convince himself that it was some sort of trick with chemicals, but he was not happy looking at it, especially when it began to coalesce into features that were not those of Sebastian Newcastle.

The face was that of a woman. Its mouth worked feebly as if it did not have the strength to speak. From somewhere came a sound that was like whispering, or the scurrying of rats. The face shifted and flickered, and sometimes it seemed to be a man with a full beard. Now there were two whispers, one lower than the other, and Callender began to believe that he could hear what they were saying. It was one word repeated over and over again: "Felicia."

Callender knew that his hands were trembling and hoped the women would not notice. The light of the glowing mist gleamed in Felicia's eyes as she leaned forward across the table. Callender was dismayed by the eagerness with which she seemed to welcome this horror, whether it was fraudulent or not. He hoped it was an illusion, for he had no wish to think it real, yet it infuriated him to realize that he could be frightened by a humbug. He closed his eyes, but the sound of the whispering, wavering voices was even more disturbing when he was blind to their source. He would have preferred to leave.

"Felicia," whispered the sibilant chorus. "Beware, daughter. Beware of false friends. There is one here whom you must not trust."

"Who is it?" asked Felicia breathlessly. She

and her aunt stared into the shifting mist.

"It is the man," the voices cried.

"Which man?"

"The man who tells you these damned lies!" shouted Callender. He pushed back his chair and pulled his hands free while the floating faces burst into brilliant light and disappeared into impenetrable darkness. He fumbled for a match as Aunt Penelope screamed.

Callender struck a light on the side of the table and applied it at once to the candle. The two women stood behind him, clutched in each other's arms, and an indistinct figure sat slumped in the medium's chair. Callender waited for another trick, fearful that the flame would be extinguished again, but there was only silence in the black room. The body of Sebastian Newcastle was ominously still.

"Is he dead?" asked Aunt Penelope.

"I hope so," muttered Callender. He walked briskly to the figure in the chair and grasped it roughly by the hair, pulling its hanging head up into the light. The features that rose up to meet him were those of his uncle William.

The waxy eyelids were closed, but the full lips moved. "Dead," said Uncle William.

Aunt Penelope gasped and swayed into the arms of her niece, who hurried the fainting woman from the room with brisk efficiency.

Callender stood as if paralyzed and stared into the face of a familiar corpse. His fingers slipped slowly from the head, and the lips twisted into a comfortable grin. When the eyes opened they were William Callender's; he might have been alive again.

"Surprised, are you, my boy? Well, there will be more surprises in store for you soon. Wait till you talk to old Frobisher tomorrow about my will!"

Callender was hardly listening, although he would have cause to remember those words soon enough. Whatever it was in the chair seemed so relaxed and genial that it convinced him more than an army of phantoms could have. "Is it really you?" he asked.

"Of course it's me!"

"Back from the dead?"

"Not so far to come, really. Takes time to travel on, you know. Especially for someone like me, who's not what you could call spiritually advanced. But this Newcastle is a very clever fellow, and he's helping me along. Don't trifle with him, my boy."

Callender had almost forgotten that he was speaking to a ghost. Everything was very natural and full of the ordinary irritations of talking with his uncle. "The man is a threat to Felicia," insisted the irate nephew. "Even the spirits of her parents told her so."

"Oh, no, my dear boy. They were talking about you."

"Me? Why should she beware of me?"

"You're not so spiritually advanced yourself, are you, Reginald? Much too interested in the pleasures of the flesh, of course, and very bad tempered on top of it. And possessive, too. I'm sure you'd make the poor girl miserable. And I'm sorry to say you're really no more than a fortune hunter. You really should be more careful. Look."

Uncle William pointed to the door, and Reginald Callender turned to find Felicia standing there. Evidently she had heard everything. Callender felt a hot flush roar up his throat as he whirled to confront his uncle, but the figure in the chair was Sebastian Newcastle, smiling with his sharp teeth and holding a pack of cards in one pale hand. "Will you have your fortune told before you go, Mr. Callender? No? Then I bid you a good evening." And with that the medium glided out of the chair and through the black velvet curtains that covered the walls.

Callender hurried to his fiancée's side. "Did you see him? Did you see Uncle William?"

Felicia nodded. "And so did Aunt Penelope. I had to help her out to the carriage, but she swears she never had such a stimulating evening in her life."

"And did you hear what he said?"

"Only what Mr. Newcastle said to you. And since he has retired, I believe we should follow his example."

Callender wondered for the first time, but not the last, if it was possible that she was mocking him. Yet he was confused enough to take her arm and walk halfway down the hall with her before he pulled away.

"He's a fraud, I tell you, and I can prove it." He hurried back into the black room, devoid of a strategy but determined to redeem himself. He glared around at emptiness and then rushed to a wall. "All tricks," he told himself. "The curtains!"

He grasped two fistfuls of midnight velvet and pulled them apart, peering fiercely through the gap, ready for almost any sight but the one that confronted him. There was no machinery, no hidden door. There was not even a wall. There was only the night, an ebony void where clouds of yellow fog obscured the stars. Callender swayed, keeping upright only because he held on to the curtains. For a moment he felt as if he were lying on his back and staring up at the sky. His head reeled.

Then he turned on his heel and walked stiffly out of the house to the carriage where the women waited.

The Inheritance

Callender would have wasted no time in visiting his uncle's solicitor in any case, but the ghostly warning he had received was so alarming that he was awake and dressed and in the offices of Frobisher and Jarndyce long before the hour of noon. He tried to convince himself that what he had seen had been a dream, or a trick, perhaps the result of mesmerism, which reportedly had the power to make a man see anything, but certainly the previous evening's entertainment was enough to make an heir curious about the terms of the will that would determine his future.

Rising early proved to be a fruitless gesture, however, since Callender was not expected until afternoon, and Clarence Frobisher had chosen to spend the morning in Chancery. A clerk left the heir apparent to cool his heels in Frobisher's dusty chambers with no company and no entertainment except a shelf of leather-bound law books. More than once Callender toyed with the idea of nipping out for a quick one, but missing his man would have been intolerable, and truth to tell, he had an almost superstitious conviction that fortune would favor him if he remained sober until the momentous meeting had been concluded.

Nothing prevented him from dozing, however, and thus his brain was as foggy as the streets of London when he opened one eye suspiciously and discovered the solicitor making his stately entrance, preceded only by a cough which might have been intended to wake his client.

Clarence Frobisher, as Callender had had occasion to observe before, was a man with a very dry manner and an equally wet face. His voice was rasping and sandy; his attitude was distant and aloof; but his brow was perpetually dabbled with perspiration, his rheumy eyes seemed always on the verge of tears, and a soiled handkerchief was never far from his dripping nose. Callender had never liked Frobisher, but he was prepared to overlook the solicitor's personal shortcomings in exchange for the speedy delivery of Uncle William's estate.

Frobisher nodded in greeting and adjusted his rusty black suit as he lowered himself into an old horsehair chair behind his heavy mahogany desk, its surface littered with papers and broken bits of sealing wax. He glanced at a document, reached for a quill pen, then seemed to recollect himself and peered at Callender over his gold-framed eyeglasses.

"Mr. Callender?"

"I've come about my uncle William's estate."

"Well, sir. You are prompt. More than prompt, I might say."

"There is no difficulty with the will, I hope?"

"Difficulty?"

"No changes?"

"Changes? Certainly not."

Reginald Callender, now a man of property, allowed himself the luxury of a sigh. Yet something continued to nag at him. Perhaps it was the expression on Frobisher's moist lips. Had it been anyone else, he would have suspected the man was smiling.

"Then I am still the sole heir?"

"Sole heir? Yes, in a manner of speaking. There are other considerations. My fee, for one."

"Well," said Callender expansively, "I hope you will be handsomely paid."

"I have seen to that. Your uncle settled with me when the will was drawn."

"Nothing else, then?"

"The funeral arrangements were the first order of business, according to your uncle's orders. He wished no expense to be spared. There is a substantial bill from Entwistle and Son, but this is a pittance compared to the cost of the marble mausoleum."

Callender, who had not even considered this, felt thousands slipping through his fingers. "But of course the estate is large enough to pay for this," he suggested nervously.

"Precisely."

"And there is nothing else?"

"Nothing."

Something in this last exchange made Callender feel hollow inside. He could not shake off the feeling that Frobisher was toying with him. He watched the handkerchief working and wondered if the solicitor was laughing behind it.

"When I say nothing else," Callender began, "I mean no other claims against my uncle's fortune."

"Precisely."

"And when you say the estate is precisely large enough . . ."

"I am speaking as plainly as I can, Mr. Callender."

Frobisher blew his nose and made a choking, wheezing sound.

"Then be plainer still, or be damned, sir! How much is left for me? Speak!"

Frobisher pocketed his handkerchief and picked up a sheet of paper. He glanced at it, blinked, and handed it to Callender. "What is left for you," he said, and paused to clear his throat, "is precisely nothing."

Callender looked at the desk, studying the grain of the wood. He found the pattern oddly intriguing; it held his attention totally for some time, long enough, in fact, for the solicitor to become somewhat alarmed.

"Mr. Callender?"

"What?"

"A glass of port, perhaps?"

Callender laughed for an instant and watched as the solicitor stepped to a sideboard and poured the wine. It struck him as really very decent of the old boy. He could hardly think of anything else except that he would be grateful for the drink, and when he gulped it down, it did restore him to a semblance of sanity. Then all at once his thoughts were racing so fast that he was almost dizzy.

"Nothing left?" he asked. "What became of it all?"

"He spent it."

"All of it? But he was worth a bloody fortune!"

"So he was, Mr. Callender. Not even the bad investments he made in India could have made a pauper of him—or should I say of you? There's still some accounting to be made in regard to that, but I doubt if you will see enough from the colonies to stand you a good dinner."

"And the rest of it?"

"As I have said. It is more common than you might suppose for an elderly man of affairs to awake one day and realize that his hours are numbered, and that the money he has struggled to accumulate has brought him very little in the way of pleasure. Faced with the choice of delighting you or delighting himself, your uncle unhesitatingly decided on the latter course. You might say that he went out in a blaze of glory. Women, of course, and quite a bit of gambling as well. I suppose if he had won, he would have been obliged to leave you something . . ."

"But to have spent so much," Callender began.

"He became quite a generous man in his last days. Quite a bit was spent on diamonds, and I personally arranged the gift of a handsome residence to one of his favorite mistresses. He also gave substantial sums to some of the household servants, the only stipulation being that they remain in service until the day after he was laid to rest. There was a man named Booth, and a housemaid; I think her name was Alice. They should be gone by now."

Callender thought back to the emptiness of the house, which he had hardly noticed in his eagerness to visit Frobisher and Jarndyce. "I should have whipped her harder," he muttered.

"I beg your pardon?"

"Nothing. At least there's still the house."

"Mortgaged to the hilt, I'm afraid. I think he meant for you to have it, but he surprised his doctors and himself by living longer than anticipated, and his funds were very low. Still, you might realize something if you can sell it before the inevitable foreclosure. And there might be a bit left over from the Indian disaster; I believe your uncle's representative is on a ship bound for England now. A Mr. Nigel Stone."

"Cousin Nigel! That idiot! No wonder everything was lost."

Frobisher consulted another document. "I understood that you were offered the post but preferred to remain in London at your uncle's expense. Is my information incorrect?"

Callender pushed himself up from his chair and strode toward the door. He threw it open, then turned for a parting shot. "Of course I'll contest the will," he said.

"And I would be happy to represent you, but I do advise against it, since you are, in fact, the sole beneficiary. The problem is that the whole estate was spent before your turn came. To spend what little you have left on legal fees would be ill advised."

"I suppose that advice is free, is it?" Callender looked around desperately. "I believe the old bastard did this just to spite me."

"I would hardly put it as bluntly as that," suggested Frobisher. "Mr. Callender! You have forgotten your stick."

Callender whirled in the doorway and stormed back into the room to retrieve his ebony walking stick. He was tempted to smash it across Frobisher's desk but managed to stop himself in time with the realization that he could hardly afford to replace it.

Reginald Callender retreated to the nearest public house and drank three glasses of neat gin in quick succession, but even that was not enough to keep his hand from trembling. He left the place and began to walk toward the house where Sally lived, trusting that the journey would enable him to collect his thoughts.

In a sense Sally Wood was his mistress, though he was hardly fool enough to imagine that he was the only man who shared her favors. It was a considerable source of pride to him, however, to reflect that he was almost certainly the only one of her lovers who had never been obliged to pay her. She liked him, apparently; it pleased Callender to believe that this was because he was more distinguished than most of the men she met at the music hall. Still, it was possible that his status as the nephew of a wealthy and elderly gentleman had something to do with Sally's attitude; Callender wondered what she would say if she were to learn that he was destitute. Not that he would tell her, of course, but providing her with little presents or even the occasional meal might soon become a problem. The real difficulty, though, lay with Felicia; the panic with which he contemplated keeping his poverty from her was what drove him toward Sally's door.

Callender possessed a key to her lodging house, but after ascending the dark stairs he felt it advisable to pause at the door to her room before entering. He listened stealthily, always conscious of the occasion when he had intruded on a scene he would have chosen not to witness, but there was no sound from inside save for a woman's voice humming a snatch of song. Callender knocked. There was a rustling from within, and then the door opened to reveal Sally, undressed except for a black corset trimmed with red silk. A hairbrush backed with mother-of-pearl was in her hand.

"Reggie! Hello, dear."

Callender's brief touch of irritation at her use of the detested pet name was soon smothered in the warmth of her embrace. Enveloped in a cloud of perfume, he maneuvered Sally back across the threshold and shut the door behind him, then kissed her ravenously while his hands crawled over her exposed flesh. After a few moments she pushed him away, gasping and laughing at the same time. "A girl needs air, you know," she said, "and a lady likes to be spoken to first."

She sent him a smile over her shoulder, then sat down at a dressing table littered with pots of paint and powder. For a time Callender was content to lounge against the wall and watch as she brushed her gleaming chestnut hair. Sally was such a contrast to Felicia: ruddy rather than pale, voluptuous rather than slender, and distinctly physical rather than spiritual. It puzzled him that somehow he was not satisfied with Sally, who seemed to offer him everything he wanted, yet he was convinced with no proof to speak of that having his way with his fiancée would be a more stimulating experience than any that Sally could provide. The physical hardly mattered, though; Felicia's fortune was sufficient to make her a suitable companion. A glance around the room was sufficient to convince Callender of that.

The cheerful disarray which might be charming in a mistress would be utterly unsuitable in a wife. The floor was dusty, the bed unmade, and every article of furniture was covered with piles of hastily discarded clothing. The general effect would have been the same, he thought, if there were an explosion in a dressmaker's shop.

A pamphlet half covered by a crumpled sheet caught his attention; he picked it up and straightened the wrinkled cover, embellished by a crude drawing of a cloaked, skeletal figure looming over a sleeping woman. Bats and gravestones decorated the lurid title: *Varney the Vampire, or The Feast of Blood.*

"Reading penny dreadfuls, Sally?"

"A girl gets bored sometimes. And it's a good story."

"It's rubbish."

"That's as may be, but it's exciting. It's

about a gent who's dead, but he comes back at night and drinks people's blood. Sneaks right into their rooms, he does, and drains 'em dry while they sleep. He bites their throats." Sally touched her own throat to emphasize the point.

"Sounds deucedly unpleasant to me," observed Callender, flipping through the pages looking for more illustrations.

"And then they turn into vampires themselves after he's done with them."

"He also seems to go about sticking logs into people," said Callender as he found a particularly lurid drawing.

"Oh, no, Reggie. That's what they have to do to kill the vampires for good and all. Pound a stick of wood right into their hearts, they do." Sally laid a dramatic hand on her own substantial bosom.

"You don't believe this nonsense, do you?"

"I don't know about that, but it's something to think about, isn't it? Besides, I like the way it makes me feel. All goose-pimply."

"Then I advise you to light a fire."

"Would you do it, Reggie dear? I've got my hands full."

"Getting ready to go out?"

"In a bit, dear. Why?"

"Because I know a better way to warm you up." Callender tossed the pamphlet back onto the bed and walked purposefully toward the dressing table. He buried his face in Sally's curly, perfumed hair and clutched one of her breasts in each hand. She arched her back, closed her eyes, and smiled as she felt his breath on her face.

"Go into a public for a drain of gin, did you?"

"Anything wrong with that?" asked Callender as he fumbled with her corset.

"You might have brought some with you."

"Aren't I intoxicating enough?"

"That you are, Reggie. It's wonderful to have a wealthy lover. Makes a girl feel special."

Callender tore at his cravat. "You'd love me without that, wouldn't you?"

"Of course I would. And I was sorry to hear about your uncle." She pushed his clumsy hands away and quickly undressed herself.

And before long they were on her bed, the forgotten copy of *Varney the Vampire* crushed beneath their thrashing bodies.

S E V E N

A Light in the Fog

A dog barked somewhere behind him as
Reginald Callender picked his way through
the dirty streets of the East End. He brushed
aside refuse with his walking stick before he
put his feet down on the muddy stones; the
walkway was thick with dead leaves, dirty
scraps of paper, and other things he did not
choose to identify. Many were malodorous.

The fog stank as well. What rose from the
river near at hand should have been clean and
gray, no more than a vapor floating above the
ancient and mighty Thames, but the water
was no purer than the air of London. The
whole city was corrupted by sewage, and
spillage, and smoke. The fog was yellow,
sometimes even brown, inspiring coughs and

gasps, and an uncomfortable redness of the eyes. Callender cursed the fog. He knew how much money its foulness brought to the men who owned the factories, but he was not one of them, and received nothing of their bounty except all the symptoms of a nasty cold.

And as if that were not enough, the fog was blinding him. Even now, before the sun had set, the neighborhood of Limehouse was dark and dim, very much as if it had come out of his mind, some ugly and unpleasant dream. He should have been happily at home, thinking only about the size of his dinner. Instead, he was wandering through the darkness, completely out of his element, in a fog in more ways than one. Shadowy figures scurried past him: a one-eyed sailor with a black patch, a woolen cap, and an old pea coat; a brown man with a turban and a broken nose.

Callender half expected to have his throat cut, and his mission to find a man he had never met began to look like madness.

It was Sally's fault, of course. Yet the information she had offered when they rose again and dressed themselves might prove to be even more to his advantage than her perfumed flesh. A woman in her position had occasion to learn much of the darker aspects of life, and he would be a fool if he did not take advantage of her information.

"You want a runner," she had said.

"And what, pray tell, is a runner?"

"A runner? That's what the police used to be before there were police. A Bow Street runner."

"You've lost me, Sal."

"Well, it was before our time, weren't it? Maybe twenty years ago. Before they opened Scotland Yard. They had these chaps then, the runners. They looked into things. The king paid 'em a guinea a week to keep an eye out, and if you wanted something special, they were yours for a guinea a day. They were detectives, like."

"And are there still some living, Sal?"

"And working, too. But not without no money from the king. What do you want one for, anyway?"

"There's a man who needs watching, Sal."

"Oh? And what does he need watching for?"

"He's an enemy. He wants my money."

"Wants your money, does he? Well, dear, we can't have that. You go see Mr. Sayer. Mr. Samuel Sayer."

That name, on the lips of a slattern, sent Callender down to the docks. He had mentioned his need for a man to look into something, and that had been enough to set Sal off, insisting that she had the very one for the job.

111

She couldn't, or wouldn't, explain where she had heard of him.

"I know what I know," she had said, and now Callender wished that she had known the man's address as well. This was the right neighborhood, unless the cabman had led him astray, but Callender's vaguely formulated plan, to seek information from the first passerby he encountered, now struck him as the height of folly and more than likely dangerous as well. As he turned toward the water, the stench grew stronger in his nostrils, and he heard the faint sound of the river lapping at the shore and flowing past the pilings. Wood creaked; there was an occasional splash or even a shout; but the Thames flowed through a sea of mist that obscured it utterly. Callender turned away with a shiver and saw that the streets behind him were almost equally shrouded. He felt the touch of panic on his shoulder. He was lost.

The only glimmer of hope he spied was the dim glow from a gaslight somewhere to his left. He moved cautiously toward it, waving his cane from side to side before him as if he were a blind man. It rattled on the pavement as he stepped ankle-deep into a puddle. He cursed, stretched out his free hand, and groped toward the light. It grew larger, brighter; then suddenly it was blotted out by a black shadow.

Callender's hand touched something that felt like a soft wall.

"Here, mate, keep 'em to yourself, will you?"

The voice was as rough as the fingers that pushed at Callender's face, sending him sprawling to the ground while cheap gin spread its perfume through the fog. Callender caught his breath, struggled to his feet, and realized that he was outside the door of a waterfront tavern.

He felt his way in. The first thing he noticed was the slant of the warped wooden floor, which nearly caused him to stumble again; he might have been on the deck of a ship. The tap room into which Callender made his way was nearly empty, or so it seemed at first. Filthy red curtains hid the windows, the walls were covered with nautical prints so stained with soot that they seemed to blend into their background, and the beams in the ceiling had been blackened with smoke. The tables were empty, and Callender was about to push through the leaded glass door into the bar, when he saw something hanging from a chair that had been placed, with its back to him, before the fireplace. What he saw was a man's hand, and there was a long clay pipe in it.

Something in this sight fascinated him. He circled the chair slowly, his head bent low, his whole body leaning forward quite unconsciously, his manner that of a hunter sneaking up on unwitting prey. The bowl of the pipe held a nugget of burning red and black that looked like a fragment of the dying fire in the grate. The man in the chair sat perfectly still. His close-cropped hair was the color of iron; his strongly seamed face looked like old leather. He was wrapped in a coat of navy blue whose cut was long out of style, and he gave every indication of being fast asleep, but as Callender moved closer, one of the man's eyelids began to quiver, then to rise in the slow and stately manner of a theater curtain. What it revealed was an eye of such a cold and piercing blue that it startled Callender into an apologetic retreat, sending him through the door of mottled blue glass and into the bar beyond.

The scene he discovered there was hardly livelier than the one he had just left behind. There was only one patron of the establishment present, a sullen, bearded fellow who stared into a half-empty pint of beer as if it contained some deep and sorry secret. The proprietor of the place, a small unshaven man with a bald head and a red face, sat in a corner under a flickering lamp. At the sound of Callender's entrance he glanced up from his newspaper, sighed heavily, carefully folded the paper to mark his place, and rose to his feet as if the weight of the world were on his shoulders.

"Gin," said Callender.

The barkeeper looked wearily around at the array of bottles and then selected one. "Lemon?" he asked.

"Lemon," said Callender. "And you might make it a double."

The barkeeper brightened at this suggestion; his lips twitched for an instant into what might have been meant for a smile, but his expression lapsed into melancholy when Callender dropped a bank note onto the surface of the stained and scarred surface of the bar.

"I don't know if we can change that, sir."

"You may not be obliged to," said Callender. He paused significantly. "I am looking for a man."

The barkeeper was so pleased at the prospect of not providing change that he began to polish Callender's glass with a corner of his soiled apron, yet the look on his face continued to be troubled.

"A man?" he said. "Not many men here now." He glanced mournfully around his sparsely populated establishment. "Might be more in tonight if this fog lifts. What would you want this man to do, sir?"

The question was offered with a leer and a

flourish of the gin bottle that reminded Callender how far out of his element he was.

"I am looking for one man in particular," he said.

"I see, sir. I beg your pardon, I'm sure. And who might that particular man be?"

"A Mr. Sayer. Mr. Samuel Sayer."

Callender's money still lay on the bar. The barman stared at it wistfully, and as Callender took a gulp of gin he noticed that the bearded beer drinker beside him had also transferred his gaze to the bank note. It was, Callender supposed, enough of a sum to interest the more common sort of man. In fact, he had intended it to do so, but he was suddenly aware of the fact that it is not always wise to attract attention. The man with the beard sidled casually toward him.

"Sayer," said the bartender, trying to look thoughtful. "Samuel Sayer. I've heard the name. Do you have business with him, sir?"

Callender was about to answer, when he noticed to his horror that his drinking companion was pulling a large and ugly knife out of his sleeve.

"I'll take care of this business myself," he growled. He raised the knife above his head.

Callender cringed as the blade flashed down, but he would not have been fast enough to avoid it if it had been aimed at him. What spared him was the fact that the blow had been directed at his five-pound note. It was pinned to the bar, and the man who claimed it still had his fingers wrapped around the hilt of his weapon.

"Maybe the gentleman would like to pay more," he whispered. His breath was foul.

"Maybe he would," said Callender's host. "Maybe he would at that. It might be worth almost anything to meet Mr. Sayer, now that you mention it."

Callender wondered if surrendering all his money would be enough, or if he would be killed no matter what he did. He imagined the man with the beard would prefer to see him safely out of the way. He wanted to strike a bargain but found that he could not speak. Through his mind flashed pictures of the people who had brought him to this sorry end: Sally, Felicia, Uncle William, and most of all Sebastian Newcastle. He hated every one of them as much as if they had conspired to murder him.

He could not help noticing, however jumbled his thoughts might be, that if he had lost his tongue, the barkeeper most certainly had not.

"That's right," the fellow babbled almost as if he were at prayer, "Mr. Sayer is the man we wants. Mr. Samuel Sayer."

He was almost shouting, and Callender noticed through his daze that the man's eyes were fixed not on the men standing before him but on the wall behind them.

While Callender stared at the barman, he felt a terrific blow on his shoulder that sent him staggering the length of the bar and crashing into the wall. He wheeled to defend himself, his walking stick instinctively raised, then froze at the sight of the tableau before him. The man from the tap room, the one with the gray hair and the piercing eye, had grasped the bearded ruffian's wrist and was slowly, inexorably, pulling his hand away from the knife that was still buried in Callender's cash.

The two men struggled silently, face-to-face, while the proprietor looked on like a referee. Callender felt an impulse to join in the struggle but checked himself with the odd conviction that his interference might be an insult to his rescuer. In any case, the stranger hardly seemed in need of help. Exerting steady pressure, he forced his opponent's hand away from the bar and down. The bearded man was gasping audibly; his eyes bulged with strain; his face was the color of a brick. All at once he collapsed, giving up the struggle like a lost cause. He dropped to his knees.

"Now, Jacky," said the man with the gray hair. "Haven't I warned you before? Surely I have?" He spoke politely, almost apologetically, but at the same time he twisted the arm he grasped until the man beneath him cried out sharply. "You must learn to ply your trade elsewhere, my lad. I can't have you disturbing my rest this way."

"I didn't know you were here. I swear it." Jacky's beard was scraping the dirty floor, his face pressed painfully against the bar's brass rail.

"No? You didn't know I was here? But you knew this young gent was a friend of mine, didn't you? You heard him ask for me. And you knew that money on the bar was mine."

"I'm sorry, Mr. Sayer. I swear it won't happen again."

"Not for some time, in any case," said Mr. Samuel Sayer. He put one muddy black boot on Jacky's shoulder and wrenched at his arm until something snapped.

Callender cringed, and the man on the floor turned suddenly pale as death. Cold sweat broke out on his face, but he stayed mute. Sayer stepped away from him.

"All right, Jacky lad. I'm done with you. Be off about your business. And be glad you've had only a broken arm instead of the broken neck you'll get when you meet the hangman. You thank your lucky stars I'm not from Scotland Yard!"

This last bit of advice was delivered in something close to a shout as Jacky scuttled from the bar cradling his crippled limb. Callender heard the outer door slam behind the injured thief. He looked at Samuel Sayer with an awe that he was at pains to conceal, convinced that it would gain him nothing to grovel. Instead, he tipped his hat, bowed slightly to Sayer, and returned to his spot at the bar. "I'm still waiting for my drink," he said. "A double gin with lemon. And another for Mr. Sayer."

"I wouldn't drink that gin if I were you," said Samuel Sayer, "but the house does have a fair bottle of peach brandy. It's sweet but soothing."

"Just as you say," Callender replied.

The shamefaced barman poured the drinks at once, placing a glass on each side of Callender's punctured five-pound note. Callender nodded down at it.

"I think that's yours," he told Sayer.

Sayer pocketed the money and dropped the knife beside his glass of brandy. "That should pay for two drinks under the circumstances," he said to the barman. "You can sell it back to Jacky if you've a mind, but you might be safer if you use it to cut your lemons."

The man said nothing as he put the knife away.

"Bring us a candle," Sayer told him. "And bring the bottle, too."

Sayer put a cordial arm around Callender's shoulder and directed him gently toward a small door at the far end of the bar. A crudely lettered sign affixed to it bore the word "Cozy."

"We'll have as much privacy here as the establishment affords," Sayer whispered. "I'm sure the proprietor will mind his manners."

The little man with the shining head pushed his way ahead of them, depositing a burning candle in a brass holder beside the stubby cordial bottle embossed with glass grapes. Then he backed silently out of the room. The table on which he had deposited the treasures was small and square; four sagging chairs surrounded it. Callender found the place less cozy than confined, but took the seat that Sayer offered him.

"State your name, please, and your business."

"My name is Reginald Callender, and I have a man who wants watching."

"Do you indeed? You have paid for five days. I hope you will not think it unjust of me if I count tonight as the first of them."

"Certainly not," said Callender, who was determined not to be intimidated. "Especially as I have further need of you tonight."

"You were well advised to come to me," Sayer said. He downed his brandy and poured himself another. In the candlelight his eyes were like glass, and the lines in his face seemed to have been carved by a chisel. "It isn't safe for a young blood like yourself to go round playing at police work."

"Acknowledged. I might have been killed if you hadn't been here. Quite a coincidence."

"I don't believe in coincidence. You found what you were looking for." Sayer took another sip of brandy, and his client followed suit. It was smooth and fragrant and sugary, and it warmed him.

"Tell me about the man," urged Sayer.

"His name is Newcastle. Sebastian Newcastle. At least that's what he calls himself. I wouldn't be surprised if even the name were a fraud."

"You may be right, but he's been using that name for several years. This is the man who talks to the dead, is it?"

"I see you really are a detective," said Callender after a pause. "How did you come to know of him?"

"A man in my line of work knows many things," Sayer replied. He looked as if he

122

meant to say no more, but then relented. "You're not the first to come to me about this Newcastle. There was a case a few years ago, in 'forty-three, I think. A man came to me who suspected your friend Newcastle of fraud."

"Fraud? Of course he's a fraud! You don't really think he can raise spirits, do you?"

Sayer sipped his brandy and stared at him over the rim of his glass. "If you're so certain he's a fraud, what need have you of me?"

"I'm not concerned with his taking pennies from widows and orphans, you know. There may be a large inheritance at stake. What did you find out about him?"

"Very little."

"Well, that's hardly encouraging, is it?"

"But hardly my fault, either. I was called off the case. That happens frequently in this business, as you might imagine."

"Oh? And why is that?"

"Might be for any number of reasons. Sometimes a client finds the expense too great."

Callender, only a few days away from penury, understood the problem all too well. He was beginning to wish he had his five pounds back.

"And sometimes," continued Sayer, "a man finds out more than he wants to know. Uncovering a secret isn't always pleasant. I can usually dig up something, but I can't make it palatable. Another factor that might stop a man from going on would be what you might call, sir, intimidation."

"You mean they're frightened off?" Callender poured himself another drink, the neck of the bottle rattling once or twice against the glass.

"Something along those lines," said Sayer.

"And could you be . . . intimidated?"

"Not as long as I'm well paid. No man has ever called me coward."

"No, of course not. I saw that. But we must talk to this fellow, the one who dropped the case."

"I'm afraid that's quite impossible. It doesn't do for me to name names, sir; it would be a breach of confidence. You, for instance, wouldn't wish for me to . . ."

"Quite so," said Callender.

"And anyway, the man is dead."

"Dead?" Callender just managed to avoid choking on his drink. "Do you mean he was murdered?"

"I couldn't say, sir. I wasn't hired to investigate, you see."

Callender sat in silence. He felt as if the walls of the tiny room were closing in on him.

"There's nothing free in this life, is there?" Sayer went on. "You can't expect to have a fine suit of clothes like yours unless you pay the tailor. An honest day's work for an honest day's pay, that's the ticket."

Callender, who had no way of paying for his new suit, was now definitely pleased that he had hired a detective. There might be more at stake than a fortune here. There might be danger for Felicia, or even for himself. He lost himself in wild speculation until Sayer pulled him back to earth.

"That brick house near the cemetery. All Souls. Is Newcastle still there?" asked Sayer.

"He is indeed. And that place needs looking into. He must have it all rigged out with machinery, to do what I've seen. He's like one of those conjurers you see at the theater. But he won't be there tonight. I'm to meet him later, along with two ladies."

"Ah." Sayer smiled, but it was not a reassuring sight. "Ladies. There's always a lady in the case. The French have a saying about it."

"I'm sure they do," Callender said stiffly. "The lady in question is my fiancée. Miss Felicia Lamb."

"I see. And the other?"

"Her aunt Penelope. She is of no consequence. But Felicia came into a considerable inheritance when she was still a child, and I believe Newcastle has designs on it. He says he can speak to her parents, and she is dangerously under his influence. She is a sensitive woman, inclined to be melancholy, and I fear he will injure her spirit unless we can expose him."

"Not to mention make off with her money."

"The money doesn't enter into it, except as his motive. My uncle William is recently deceased, and I am his heir. My only concern is for Felicia."

"Have you considered calling in Scotland Yard?"

"This must be a private matter. Felicia might misunderstand if she knew of our investigations before we could show her what manner of man he is."

"You interest me strangely, Mr. Callender. I'll take your case."

"I assumed you took it when you took my five pounds."

"Just so, just so. And where will this meeting be tonight?"

"At Madame Tussaud's, Baker Street. But surely you won't follow us there when his house will be empty?"

"And how do you know the house will be empty?" Sayer rose from his chair. "You must leave these things to me, Mr. Callender. For now, let me find you an honest cabman who will see you safely home."

"But how will I find you again?"

"This is as good a place as any. I'm often here when I'm not on a job."

"I don't even know where I am, to tell you the truth. It's this damned fog."

"This is The Black Dog. You can see the sign on a clear day. It doesn't look much like a dog, but it's black enough."

"Don't you have rooms somewhere?"

"Somewhere that I keep hidden. A man in my position must keep his bed under wraps, so to speak. Don't concern yourself, Mr. Callender. When there's need of it, I'll find you."

EIGHT

The Dead Room

The parade of kings stood still and a common man marched past. He was a guide, dressed in a uniform that made him look like a soldier, and he announced each crowned head of Europe in a hoarse voice that Callender found increasingly irritating. He was thoroughly sick of the officious little man and his apparently endless procession of wax effigies; his dislike of these soft statues and their false finery had begun before he had even entered Madame Tussaud's, when he had been informed that due to the flammable nature of the exhibits, he would be obliged to throw away the last of his uncle William's imported cigars.

And nothing before or after this affront had been calculated to soothe Callender's temper.

The expedition to Madame Tussaud's exhibition had begun disastrously when the cab Callender had hired had arrived at Felicia Lamb's residence only to find her absent. Aunt Penelope, however, had been obtrusively present, coquettishly claiming Callender as her escort with the explanation that Mr. Newcastle, the medium, had taken Felicia into his coach a quarter of an hour before. Callender's initial indignation had rapidly given way to a feeling close to panic; he could not quite suppress the unreasonable fear that his fiancée had been abducted and he would never see her again. The journey to the wax museum, accompanied by Aunt Penelope's incessant chatter, had been excruciating.

The upshot, which surprised him by irritating him, had been nothing at all. Felicia, eyes downcast demurely, had stood in the gaslit lobby of the Baker Street Bazaar, and she had been holding Sebastian Newcastle's long, thin arm. This apparent intimacy, combined with the anticlimax of it all, left Callender fuming, and as Aunt Penelope pulled him toward the exhibition, he thought he saw Felicia smile gratefully at her. Apparently Newcastle had paid for all their tickets, and there was nothing that Callender could reasonably be expected to do about that.

Callender's tour of the wax museum had

become a nightmare long before he reached the Chamber of Horrors. He hardly noticed the exhibits, but he did not miss a single one of the glances exchanged between his fiancée and Sebastian Newcastle. They seemed to be hanging back deliberately, engaged in private conversation, while Callender was pushed forward by the press of the crowd and by Aunt Penelope, a woman he would willingly have strangled. Callender's face was hot, and his cravat was choking him: Was it possible that Felicia was deliberately snubbing him? He was so intent on the couple behind him that he nearly knocked over the guide when the procession suddenly came to a halt in front of a door barred by a red velvet rope.

"This concludes the tour of the exhibition," announced the little man in the blue uniform. "The general exhibition, that is. But behind me, ladies and gentlemen, behind this rope, behind this door, stands the Dead Room, or, as some have been generous to call it, Madame Tussaud's Chamber of Horrors. Those of you who have purchased tickets for this special display may follow me now, but I caution you that this is a room filled with effigies of evil and engines of extermination. Here are the most notorious murderers and malefactors of history and of the present day, together with authentic devices of torture and execution, including the very guillotine that killed the king of France. In addition, you will see replicas of the severed heads of the king and his queen, Marie Antoinette, along with those of such notables as Mr. Robespierre, all of them authentic impressions taken immediately after decapitation by the fair hands of Madame Tussaud when she was but a young girl, more than half a century ago. This is not an exhibit for the faint-hearted, ladies and gentlemen, but you have been warned, and those of you who are willing to brave the Dead Room will now please follow me."

Callender watched in some surprise as the crowd melted away; whether they were prudent or merely parsimonious, the British public did not seem inclined, at least on this night, to feast on horrors. In fact, there were finally only four customers, and they were all of Callender's party. Aunt Penelope uttered a little cry of excitement as the portal to the Chamber of Horrors opened to admit her.

The room was dark, deliberately thought Callender, and his first impression was of a crowd of men waiting in the shadows. As his eyes became accustomed to the lack of light, he realized that the figures had been grouped like prisoners waiting for sentence in the dock. There were women scattered among the men; an ancient woman in a gray gown particularly caught his eye. In general, though, they seemed to be a nondescript lot, and only statues anyway.

"So this is the celebrated Dead Room," boomed Callender, conscious that Felicia was following him. "It doesn't look that frightening. I'd gladly take the hundred guineas to spend a night among these frozen fiends."

"Sorry, sir," replied the smiling guide. "Dame Rumor offered that reward, not Madame Tussaud, who has no wish for visitors after we close our doors at night at ten o'clock. The only living human being allowed to spend the night among these figures is Madame Tussaud herself."

"Would you really have done it, Reginald?" gasped Aunt Penelope, and Callender was conscious of a certain satisfaction, even though he would have preferred to elicit such a response from Felicia. He risked a glance backward, and was pleased to see her pale blue eyes upon him.

"Of course, the story of the reward is a lie," he said. "There's nothing here to scare a schoolboy. Who are those two fellows?" He gestured with his stick at a pair of shaggy ruffians bedecked in caps and ragged scarves.

"Well, sir, you're taking them out of order, but since there are so few of you tonight, I don't suppose it matters. These two are Burke and Hare. Ghouls, grave robbers, and murderers, who stole bodies for a doctor's dissecting lessons, then turned to killing when the supply of fresh corpses ran short. Burke was executed in 1829 on his partner's evidence. They stole dignity from the dead and breath from the living. A most despicable pair, and one of our most popular groupings."

The story, which reminded Callender of something in his recent past, did not amuse him. "Of course this sort of thing is far behind us," he observed, "now that we provide our medical schools with the specimens they need."

"Yet still there are vermin who would rob the dead," said Sebastian Newcastle. Callender's hand moved involuntarily toward the pocket of his waistcoat and toward his uncle William's watch. He wondered again how much power the medium might possess, then shook off his suspicions together with his memories of the séance. That vision had been the result of hypnotism, or fatigue, or perhaps of some drug, but it certainly had nothing to do with the supernatural.

"Surely no man could be so contemptible," murmured Felicia, and again Callender felt a flush of shame. Could they know? He remembered a line from an old play his uncle had dragged him to see, about conscience creating cowards, and he kept his peace. Yet it disturbed him to realize that neither Sebastian Newcastle nor Felicia Lamb had spoken a word to him outside of perfunctory greetings until the subject of rifling corpses had arisen. He looked desperately for a diversion and found one he could hardly have hoped for when Felicia's Aunt Penelope began to scream.

His eyes followed her pointing finger, then widened in shock when he saw what she had seen first. It was the old woman in gray, half hidden among the murderers. She rose. Her wrinkled face turned toward the dim gaslight, and her eyes gleamed as a small smile twisted her wizened features. A gigantic shadow rose behind her as she stood, and Callender stumbled backward as Aunt Penelope collapsed into his arms. They both would have fallen to the floor but for the cold, rigid bulk of Mr. Newcastle. Callender felt Newcastle's hand close on his flailing wrist, and suddenly he was less afraid of the walking effigy than of the icy presence behind him. He saw in flashes the cold face of Newcastle, the contemptuous countenance of Felicia, and the wrinkled features of the old woman that glided toward him.

"Madame Tussaud!" said the guide, scuttling back in a broad gesture that was equally composed of bowing and cringing. "I didn't expect you here!"

"You all but announced me, Joseph. And where else would a crone like me find her friends except among the dead? You may leave early tonight, Joseph; I shall be hostess to our guests. There is one among them who interests me."

Joseph virtually fled. Callender whipped his head around, expecting to find the eyes of the old waxworker focused on him, but Madame Tussaud was blinking intently at Sebastian Newcastle.

"Have we not met, sir?"

"I hardly think I could have encountered Madame without remembering her."

"You are gracious, but are you truthful?"

Madame Tussaud's English, however fluent, still betrayed her French upbringing, and there was something foreign in Newcastle's speech as well, but Callender could not identify it.

"You have a memorable face, I think," said the old woman.

"Now you flatter me," said Newcastle.

"That was hardly my intention, but your scar, if I may be so blunt, is all but unforgettable."

"I apologize if it affronts you."

"No, sir. It is I who should beg your pardon,

but I think I remember you. One who has lived eighty-seven years, as I have, has seen much. And it seems to me that I recollect a man with a face like yours, or at least talk of him. But that was so many years ago that the man could hardly have been you."

Sebastian Newcastle contented himself with a bow. The Dead Room was so dark, and their faces so indistinct, that Callender could hardly tell what the two of them were thinking. More than anything, he was aware of the way Felicia's eyes shifted back and forth between the two. What really shocked him, though, was the sudden recovery of Aunt Penelope, who pulled herself out of his arms and demanded to know whether the two of them were acquainted or not.

"There were stories in Paris, when the revolution raged," said Madame Tussaud, "about a magician, one who had found a way to keep himself alive forever."

"No doubt there were many such stories in a time of turmoil," said Newcastle.

"Of course," agreed Madame Tussaud. "And the man I speak of would have been older then than I am now. This was more than fifty years ago. It can be no more than a coincidence."

"Men say that there are such things," said Newcastle.

"He was a Spaniard," said Madame Tussaud, "and I would have given much to model him in wax, but that is all behind us now. Will you look at my relics of the revolution? I paid dearly for them."

"How so?" asked Felicia. Fascinated by the exchange between the others, Callender had almost forgotten her.

"With the blood on my hands, young lady, and with memories that will last as long as this old body holds them. I was apprenticed to my uncle, and the leaders of the revolution ordered me to make impressions in wax of heads fresh from the basket of the executioner. Fresh from the blade of that!"

Madame Tussaud thrust her arm out dramatically. Her trembling finger pointed toward a looming silhouette of wooden beams and ropes. Even in the dim light the slanted steel blade at the top gleamed dully.

"The guillotine," gasped Aunt Penelope.

She swayed toward it slowly, like a woman in a trance, and stared up at the sharp edge as if she expected it to shudder down and smash into its base at her approach. She lowered her eyes gradually, then bent over to examine the displays at the foot of the guillotine. She looked to Callender like a housekeeper examining the choice cuts in a butcher shop.

The waxy heads gazed up reproachfully, their indignation threefold: bad enough to have been cut off, worse yet to have been captured in wax, but unsupportable to be displayed to gawkers at a penny apiece. Aunt Penelope seemed to wilt under their gaze. She made a strange sound.

"I don't feel well at all," she said. "I think I should go home."

"We should all go," said Callender.

"No, no, my boy, I wouldn't think of it. Mr. Newcastle is Madame Tussaud's old friend. You take me, and let the others stay." Aunt Penelope began to sway toward Callender's arms again, a habit which was becoming increasingly annoying.

"It's very good of you, Reginald," added Felicia with sweet finality. "I shall be quite safe here with Mr. Newcastle."

Callender was sorely tempted to disagree, but he sensed the futility of argument. There was very little choice for anyone who wanted to look like a gentleman except to carry the old fool out and find her a cab. He tried to maintain his composure while he backed clumsily out of the Dead Room as the three who stayed behind smiled at him; he might not have succeeded if he had seen Aunt Penelope winking at her niece.

"Evidently age brings wisdom even to a woman such as she," Newcastle remarked.

"She's such a dear, really, although she does rattle on sometimes. She knew how much I wanted to remain a little longer, and Reginald would have been bound to cause a scene of some sort."

"Then you wish to see more of my handiwork?" asked Madame Tussaud.

"No," Felicia replied at once. "I mean yes, of course, but I really wanted to hear more about the gentleman you spoke of, the one who was so like Mr. Newcastle."

"He might have been an ancestor, perhaps," suggested the man with the scar.

"And are such wounds as this passed on from father to son?" asked the old woman. She reached up and caressed Newcastle's cheek. "I could wish to make a model of such a face."

"For your Dead Room, Madame?" Newcastle asked.

"Mr. Newcastle is no stranger to the dead," Felicia said. "He speaks to them. He is a spiritualist." She felt that she had to say something, even though a mixture of common courtesy and uncommon fear kept her from posing the question she longed to ask. There was some sort of understanding between these two, and she was impatient to share it.

"This gentleman from Paris," she said at last. "Do you remember his name?"

The old woman smiled and put her hand to her temple. "He was a Spanish nobleman . . . Don Sebastian . . . can you help me, Mr. Newcastle?"

"I believe I can. I have made a study of such things. His name was Don Sebastian de Villanueva, but I also recall that any claim he had to immortality was false. Was he not reported dead?"

The old woman thought for a moment. "A girl was found, driven quite out of her wits, who said she saw him shatter like glass, or vanish in a puff of smoke, or some such thing, so I suppose he is dead. Then again, a master of the black arts might be capable of such tricks if he found it convenient to disappear for a time . . ."

"Quite so," said Sebastian Newcastle, and Felicia Lamb shivered. From somewhere nearby she heard the tolling of a bell.

"The hour grows late," said Madame Tussaud, "and I am an old woman. I must ask you to leave me alone among my friends."

"Indeed, Madame," said Newcastle. He drew a silver watch from his waistcoat and glanced at its face. The watch was shaped like a skull. "The time is late, the museum is closed, and a man in my position must never be accused of keeping a young lady out till an indecent hour. We must take our leave. Good night, Madame."

The waxworker curtsied, the medium bowed, and Felicia felt herself being hurried from the Dead Room. As soon as she was through the door, Newcastle paused.

"Please wait here. I must return for a few seconds. I neglected to pay our guide for our tour."

Madame Tussaud was waiting for him in the shadows by the guillotine. "Don Sebastian," she said.

"Madame," he replied. "I trust you to keep my secret."

"You can hardly expect to keep it much longer from that girl, you know."

"It matters little. She will become a disciple. She wishes it."

"And has she said as much?"

"She need not speak for me to know."

"And have you many such disciples after half a century in London?"

"None," said Don Sebastian. He gazed at the wax figures around him. "But I have my dead, like you, and also those who will pay to see them. A small income, but my needs are simple."

"I think you need something that you cannot buy with gold, do you not?"

"Gold will buy more than you think, sometimes. And when it will not, I feed as lightly as I can, so that my prey knows nothing more than a few days of weakness, soon forgotten. I never drink from the same fountain twice. I rarely forget myself enough to dine too heavily, and if I do, well, there is a remedy for that."

"A physic made of wood, perhaps?"

"You are wise, Madame."

The old woman shuffled over to a rocking chair that sat in a corner. "If eighty-seven years have not made me wise, sir, then what can I hope for?"

"I had forgotten myself, Madame. Twice I have been driven back into the world of spirits, and so my years on earth have been scarcely more than yours."

"And did you never find peace?"

"Once, when an ancient world came to an end, its gods took me to their paradise, but after some centuries a spell of my own devising drew me back to earth again, to your Paris. And since I know how many less pleasant realms there are where spirits dwell, I am content to remain here."

The old woman settled back in her chair. "Then I wish you good night, sir, and bon voyage."

"I have forgotten one thing," said Don Sebastian. He raised his arm, and a shower of

143

golden guineas streamed from his empty hand into the basket that contained the wax remains of Marie Antoinette.

"Very prettily done, sir," said Madame Tussaud, "but I hope you have not damaged that head!"

"I would not dream of such a thing, Madame. You are an artist!"

NINE

The Black Dog

Reginald Callender held himself in check for as long as he could, but little enough time passed before he felt compelled to pay another visit to The Black Dog. Three days of silence were all that he could tolerate from Mr. Samuel Sayer.

Callender had begun to consider himself the victim of a conspiracy. In only a few days he had been banned from his club, he had been disinherited, and he had found his betrothal undermined. It had done nothing to restore his spirits when Felicia's servants informed him that their mistress was in the country visiting an ailing acquaintance, and even Sally Wood was pleading previous engagements, perhaps in a childish effort to pique his interest. Callender's only companions had been the pawnbrokers, and he was convinced that they were deceiving him, too.

And so the thought that Samuel Sayer had bilked him of his five pounds and vanished into the shadows of Limehouse was more than Callender could bear. Still, neither his suspicion nor his indignation waxed strong enough to drive him back to that low tavern after sunset. Instead, he set out in the early afternoon, and although he was too ignorant of his own city's topography to deny himself the luxury of a cab, he broke precedent by taking note of the route he took: Empty pockets would oblige him to walk home whether he found Sayer or not.

Fog still infested the riverbank, but shafts of sunlight shone through the clouds, and the effect reminded Callender of old pictures he had seen of heaven. By day the streets of the neighborhood bustled with figures that seemed more colorful than menacing: fishmongers, rowdy sailors, roguish whores, and scampering children. Even The Black Dog was curiously nondescript when finally he discovered it, a ramshackle little building with a pathetic painted sign rather than that looming shape in an impenetrable mist that had rescued him, then threatened him, then rescued him again.

Something in all this cheered him immeasurably, especially when he gazed at the comical figure of an ebony hound that someone had scrawled on the tavern's sign, swaying in the faint breeze that wafted from the Thames. He felt as if a shadow had been lifted from him. If this scene, once so dreadful, could be reduced to the commonplace, might it not follow that all his other fears could be exorcised with equal efficiency? Callender decided that his trip would be worthwhile whether he found the old detective or not. With a feeling of self-confidence he had not known for days, he strolled into The Black Dog.

Lounging in a chair before the fire was the grizzled, angular figure of Samuel Sayer.

Callender was too startled to be pleased. He had expected nothing more than a chance to leave a note with the barman, certainly not the opportunity to meet Sayer face-to-face. He hardly knew what to say, and while he struggled to find words, he realized that the man he had hired was asleep.

Callender was not happy about this.

"So this is what became of the famous Bow Street runners," he muttered. "It's not much wonder they were replaced by Scotland Yard."

Callender took a stand between the detective and the fireplace, put his hands on his hips, and placed his feet well apart. This was his standard posture for chastising an inefficient servant, and it seemed appropriate enough, at least while Sayer was unconscious, though Callender had the uneasy feeling that the man in the chair before him might be about to open one of his cold blue eyes.

That didn't happen, however. Instead, Callender's reverie was interrupted by Sayer's low, hoarse voice. "Your man Newcastle sleeps by day, as nearly as I can see. And so, if I'm to follow him, must I."

Callender found that he had nothing to say.

His companion, however, gave every impression of being completely in command of the situation, though he retained the appearance of peaceful slumber. "You might go into the bar," he suggested, "and ask for a couple of peach brandies. Tell him they're for me. He won't charge you for them."

"You act as if you owned the place," said Callender with some resentment.

"I wouldn't want that widely known," Sayer replied. He was as inanimate, and yet as vocal, as a ventriloquist's dummy. "Be good enough to join me in a glass, Mr. Callender."

"But what have you discovered about Newcastle?"

"All in good time. My throat needs lubricating."

Resigned to his fate, but nonetheless resentful of it, Callender walked stiffly through the

148

glass doors that separated the tap room from the bar within. It was something less than comforting to find a tray laden with two glasses and the bottle of peach brandy laid out in front of the bald barman.

"Good afternoon, sir," the fellow said.

Two sailors at the bar, dressed in dark clothes and rough woolen caps, looked ostentatiously away from him, and Callender had the feeling that every soul on the premises knew all about him and his business. A high-pitched squeal of laughter from behind the door of the cozy did nothing to reassure him. He picked up the tray with all the dignity he could muster and, feeling very much like one of the servants he could no longer afford to keep, marched back into the tap room, where Samuel Sayer waited for him.

Sunlight made the filthy red curtains seem to glow, and stray beams caught motes of dust as they drifted around the room. Stains showed clearly on the nautical prints that adorned the walls, and the bare floorboards were sticky with the stale beer whose scent provided the establishment's dubious atmosphere.

"The Black Dog," sneered Callender as he placed the drinks on a table beside the still-somnolent Sayer.

"And what do you expect? The Red Waistcoat?"

Sayer sat up and regarded Callender with an icy eye.

"That used to be our badge, you know. A runner was like a robin redbreast. And I suppose there was some pride in announcing who we were, but it would be no more than foolishness now, when we have no standing with the government. Pull up a chair, young man."

Callender obeyed and found to his surprise that he was pouring the drinks.

"You really don't know who I am," asked Sayer, "do you?" Still slumped, he reached out a hand for his glass of sweet peach brandy. "You don't know what it meant to be a Bow Street runner."

"I suppose not," Callender allowed.

"We were the wall between gentlemen like you and the rabble all around, and we got little enough for it but the chance to be one step above the rabble, which is where we came from, truth to tell. If I hadn't served your kind, I might have slaughtered you. Understand?"

"I suppose so," ventured Callender.

"Not bloody likely. What is it that sets one man above another, eh? And why should the man below abide it? Tell me that!"

"It's just the nature of things," Callender began.

"Oh, I'm sure it seems natural enough when you've won the toss, but what's that to the man who has your boot in his face?" Sayer downed his drink and gave a shudder. "You might be right, though. The Frenchies had a revolution, didn't they, and the Americans, too, but you can bet the rich still rule. What difference does a title make? What price nobility?"

"I couldn't say. I have no title."

"No. And you don't need one, do you, as long as you've got the money."

"Well," said Callender. "You're getting mine."

"Not enough of it. It wouldn't mean a thing to you to pay twice as much, or ten times as much, but there are other men who'd take your job at your price if I didn't."

"And I'd be a fool to pay more than I needed to."

"Granted, if you'll admit that a man is entitled to take all he can get. Yet that's what made an end to the Bow Street runners. We got above our station. You don't know who we really were, do you, Mr. Callender? We were the companions to kings."

"Very likely, I'm sure," said Callender, pouring his companion another drink, "but what has this to do with me? You seem to have done quite well."

Suddenly Sayer was on his feet, his face pale. He lifted his hand as if he intended to strike Callender, or else to knock the glasses from the tray. "You call this doing well? Scraping out a bare pittance by risking my life every day? I'm not a young man, and I'm still dependent on the likes of you."

"Surely this has nothing to do with the business at hand," suggested Callender. "What have you learned about Miss Lamb? And what have you learned about Sebastian Newcastle?"

"You'll hear that when I'm ready to tell you, unless you'd rather not hear it at all. There's a story in your case worth telling, but there's another story I want you to hear first, and I trust you to bear with me, Mr. Callender, sir. You didn't go to Scotland Yard. You knew they wouldn't suit you. And now I want you to know what manner of man it is who does fulfill your needs. What do you know of the Bow Street runners?"

"Damned little," said Callender as he settled into a chair. "But I gather I'll know a great deal more before long. What were they, a race of schoolmasters?"

"We had something to teach the world, I'll say that. A pup like you has no idea what London was like before there was such a thing as a Bow Street runner. Nobody to enforce the law at all, unless you count the old parish watchmen walking through the streets shouting 'Two o'clock and all is well' whether it was or not. The watch was made up of antiquated pensioners, and they were good for nothing but running away at the first sign of a crime. Young bloods like you would knock 'em down just for the sport of it, and that was all the law there was in London until the Fieldings became magistrates at Bow Street. There were two of 'em, brothers. Henry and John. One of 'em wrote books, and the other one was blind, but whatever else was wrong with 'em, they had sense enough to know that you fight fire with fire. They brought in men who were as sly and strong and ruthless as the thieves and murderers they were hired to catch. The Bow Street runners. And I was one of 'em! Here, have another dram."

Sayer refilled their glasses, and Callender felt obliged to provide some sort of a response, if only to move the conversation along to the point where it might touch on his own interests. "What happened?" he asked lamely.

"What should have happened! We were the scourge of the underworld, my boy, so good at what we did that some people grew frightened of us. They said we were undisciplined. They said we were corrupt. A rough and ready lot, we were, I'll grant you, but what would you have? Everyone was frightened of us because we did great things."

"Frightened?" asked Callender. "Of what?"

"Of whatever they dreamed up. In Parliament they said we were undisciplined, and unreliable as well. Sir Robert bloody Peel. He didn't want men, he wanted a machine, and finally he got it. The Metropolitan Police. Scotland Yard. They came in almost twenty years ago, and their first order of business was to squeeze all of us out. Not efficient, they said. We kept our own hours, we reported to nobody. And if we lived with the thieves, why, that's how we caught 'em. Look at you. Did you go to the Yard? You don't want a man in a blue suit marching up and down in front of this Newcastle's house, do you? You want a man as sly as he is. Someone who'll get to know him like a brother. Befriend him if need be. That's why you came to me."

"I suppose so. And what have you found out?"

Sayer sat back in his chair, his eyes closed and his hands folded. "Let me ask you a question," he said. "Suppose you'd been robbed. A great sum of money. It might be, say, ten thousand pounds. No one knew anything about it. And then you hired a man to get it back. A Bow Street runner it might be, working for a pound a day. Now, some people might say that you wanted justice. You wanted the men who did it taken into custody and hanged. Is that about right?"

"Well . . . of course."

"Wrong," said Samuel Sayer. "I put it to you that what you really want is to get your money back. You don't want to meet these fellows, and you don't care if they live or die. What you care about is your ten thousand pounds."

"I suppose you're right," admitted Callender. "But how will I get it if the men aren't caught?"

"Ah. That's where I come in. Or, that is to say, a man in my profession. You pay me a pound a day to look into the matter. Of course I'd still have my pound a week from the government, but that's hardly enough, and anyway, I'd be working to see justice done. It might take a long time. Your man would have to infiltrate the gang, so to speak, following rumors and storing up evidence. It might take weeks, even months. It might cost you hundreds of pounds. But suppose at the end of it that your man had these thieves dead to rights. He could go to them, suitably armed, of course, and explain that he was all that stood between them and the gallows. He could demand the money back in exchange for their lives. Now, he might not get all of it. Some of it would be lost, or squandered. But he might get back most of it, and return it to you, no questions asked and no lives lost. Say six or seven thousand pounds. And all you'd pay him would be the hundred or two he'd earned. Wouldn't you think that a good bit of business?''

"Six thousand?" Callender brooded. "Then what happened to the other four thousand?"

"My God!" barked Sayer, smashing his fist down on the table in front of him so that the glasses and the brandy bottle jumped. "You're like every other man with money! You buy six thousand for two hundred and you're suspicious because you didn't get more!"

Callender hardly knew what to say. The man's indignation embarrassed him.

"I know what you'd do," snarled Sayer. "You'd grow suspicious of the man you hired, and you'd end up accusing him of stealing the money that was still missing, and you'd forget all about what you did get back. You'd stir up a scandal, you'd demand reforms, and you'd try to make a criminal out of the man who got you six thousand for two hundred. I'd call that a nice bit of business, but you'd call it graft and corruption, wouldn't you? You'd disgrace the man who served you, and try to drive him out of work. You'd back the idea of Scotland Yard, and a system that would hang the thieves and give you nothing back but the cold comfort of knowing they were hanged. I've dealt with your kind before, and you want a lot for your five pounds!"

The detective relaxed abruptly and took a sip of brandy, giving Callender the odd impression that he had just witnessed something of a performance, an oft-repeated tale that served a purpose he could not discern. He understood it just enough to detect a note of menace in it.

"Look here," he said. "All that has nothing to do with me. I'm not expecting you to recover money or capture thieves. I paid you to keep an eye on this man Newcastle and see what you could learn."

"And so I have, Mr. Callender. And you have two more days of surveillance coming. I expect that will be the end of it, though."

"What do you mean? Haven't you found out anything?"

"I've found out enough to know that you can't afford much more of my services."

"God damn your eyes," said Callender quietly.

"Don't be like that, sir. Have another drink. It's merely a matter of business."

"Business! I give you money and you use it to investigate me! I call that damned indecent."

"I'm only protecting myself, Mr. Callender, and if I've deceived you, then you deceived me first. Imagine telling me that you were the heir to a fortune! You can see why it's always in my best interest to see how the land lies. And I really didn't use your money to look into your affairs. Your legacy will be a matter of public record in a few days, and a man in my line of work always has friends in the legal profession."

Reginald Callender sat stunned. He heard laughter from the bar. "Frobisher," he said.

"It wasn't your uncle's solicitor. He's quite a circumspect man. But these documents must be copied and filed and registered. They pass through many hands, you see."

Callender slumped in his seat.

"You mustn't take it so hard. There's many a young gentleman been in your position and gone on to happiness. Just marry the girl, and you'll control her fortune. She won't even know whose money is whose, and I can assure you that her position is financially sound. Very sound indeed. It's a pity that your time and money are so short. Surely you can scare up a few more pounds with loans of some kind? Even your stick might fetch a few bob. It wouldn't do to lose everything at the last minute, would it?"

Callender reached for the bottle of brandy and filled his glass so carelessly that it overflowed. "I can't see why I should pay you any more," he said, "when you've done nothing with what I've already given you."

"That's where you're wrong, sir. An honest day's work for an honest day's pay, that's my motto. In this case, though, as I told you, most of the work has been at night. Your money hasn't been wasted. In fact, truth to tell, I've discovered a few things that should please you."

"Tell me," said Callender. He downed his drink.

"Well, first and foremost: the night you called on me. There's good news there. I followed Newcastle to Miss Lamb's house, and saw him take her away in a coach. I kept a sharp eye on them, you may be sure, but they only kept their rendezvous with you at Madame Tussaud's. I thought it more discreet to wait outside that establishment in spite of the discomfort, and I must confess I was surprised to see you drive up with a much older lady. The aunt, I suppose?"

"Just so. That was hardly my plan, but Newcastle fooled me."

"I dare say. Of course I was even more surprised, an hour later, to see you come out again with this Aunt Penelope, leaving your fiancée alone with Newcastle."

"I know. The old fool fainted, and I was stuck with her. What could I do?"

"Perhaps you should have hired me to investigate the aunt instead of Newcastle!" Sayer laughed briefly. "I followed the others when they left. Miss Lamb and Mr. Newcastle."

"And they did?"

"That's my point, and I hope it's pleasing. They did nothing."

Callender looked hard at the detective. "Could you be a little plainer?" he asked.

"I'm a plain man, Mr. Callender, and I mean just what I say. He drove her home, escorted her to her door with a great show of courtesy, and left her there. Nothing happened between them."

"Of course it didn't! Miss Lamb is pledged to marry me!"

"Just as you say, Mr. Callender."

"I never imagined that she'd be fool enough to love such an odious man, and a foreigner at that. I believe his designs are on her fortune, not her person."

"It might be both, you know. The lady is a looker."

"You've been paid to watch Newcastle, not my fiancée," rasped Callender. "Have you been following her?"

"Not at all. I've been busy with this medium of yours."

"Then you don't know where she's been for the last two days?"

"No. But I don't think she's been with

Newcastle. I've kept close watch on him."

"And how long did she spend with him at Madame Tussaud's?"

"Only a few minutes, and in a public place. Not much to fear there, I'll warrant."

"Every minute he spends with her might be dangerous. I'm convinced he means to turn her against me. And I know he's after her money. What else have you found out?"

Sayer smiled with grim satisfaction. "Something else happened that night, after I took up my post outside Newcastle's house, but there's more to that part of the story, so I'll save it for last, especially as it might be promising. As for the rest, Newcastle appears to be a man of regular habits. Unusual, but regular. He never goes out by day and receives no visitors then, either. I've made inquiries in the neighborhood, and he seems to live entirely by night. He receives people throughout the evening. His clients, you might call 'em. There's quite a list, but I made special note of one. A Miss Hazard."

"And what was so different about her?" asked Callender.

"It wasn't a difference that drew me so much as a similarity. I was looking for what you might call a pattern. Miss Hazard is also a pretty young lady, and quite well off. Not as wealthy as Miss Lamb, but her father is a prominent physician. She had a young man who died not long ago. Went west to America, the fool. And since she's been grieving for him, she sought out this Sebastian Newcastle. I arranged to meet with her, and what I found out was surprising."

"He's been cheating her, too!" exclaimed Callender.

"That's what I hoped for. These confidence tricksters often have more than one iron in the fire. Well, this Miss Hazard writes for the newspapers, if you can believe such a thing. Stories about women's rights, whatever those may be, and one about spiritualism. So I presented myself to her yesterday as a widower in search of consolation, as it were, and I asked about this Newcastle."

Callender was so intent that he had forgotten about the brandy, but he attempted to restrain himself. "Was she helpful?"

"I'd have to say yes and no at the same time. She was reassuring, if you're concerned about Miss Lamb, but not much help in damning Newcastle. In fact, she spoke of him as if he were a saint. She recommends him highly."

"Then he's fooled her, too," said Callender.

"That's as may be, sir, but I think he's done her good, and it's cost her next to nothing. She's been visiting him for almost a year, and in that time she says she's seen the spirit of her young man several times. The strange thing is that both this spirit, if it is one, and Newcastle himself have urged her to forget about the past and go on with her life as best she can. She said he's done so much for her that she doesn't expect to go to see Newcastle again, almost like he was a lawyer who'd won her case, or a doctor who had cured her. It almost made me wonder if he might not be a dedicated man."

"Impossible," said Callender.

The old detective took a tobacco pouch from his pocket and stood to retrieve a clay pipe from the mantel. When the pipe was filled and lit, he returned to his chair and began again.

"Then if you'd rather go on with this than have your two pounds back again," he said, "there is the matter of the boy."

"Boy? What boy?"

"As I've said, I've haven't seen Newcastle leave the house since that first night, and everyone who came to him seemed to be there with regard to his normal business. Except for this boy. It was about an hour before dawn, I'd say, when I saw a lad of fourteen or so approach the house. Slinking toward it, almost. He looked like a common street boy, not well dressed, and not likely to be looking for a medium. It was dark, but I think his hair might have been red."

"Well?"

"Well, sir, he behaved most oddly. Here it was after four in the morning, and damned cold, too, I'll tell you, but he went up and knocked on the door. And he did it strangely. He acted like he was afraid to be seen, but still he knocked. He hid in the shadows, and then he knocked again. And when no one answered him, he went around and rattled the windows and made some sort of moaning noises. I think he said something, but I couldn't make it out. He went around and around that house for half an hour, like he knew someone was inside who should have answered him. And Newcastle was there, I'm sure of it, but he never showed himself. And then, all of a sudden, a panic seemed to come upon the lad, and he ran away."

"You followed him, I hope."

"Yes. I hated to leave the house, but this looked like it might be something, so I took off after him, but it was no good. The sun was almost up, but the fog was thick, and he was fleet of foot. I'm sorry to say I lost him."

Callender was too discouraged to even speak.

"But there's more," Sayer reassured him. "The lad was back the next night, and his behavior was the same. Round the house, knocking, rattling, and wailing. There was something eerie about it, almost like he was a ghost. But he was solid enough, sir. And what's more, this time, even though it was so late, Newcastle let him in. And I haven't seen the boy since. What do you make of that, sir?"

"I'd rather hear your theories."

"Well, they evidently know each other, and the boy has some claim on Newcastle, but it's not welcome. He might be a relative. Wouldn't it be a nice tale for your young lady if this spiritualist had a young son that he'd abandoned? That might do you nicely! Of course there's another reason why he might have young boys in the house at night, if you get my meaning, but it wouldn't be something we could go to her about. Still, we could use it as an opportunity to warn this Newcastle away."

"This sounds more like it," Callender said.

"And I'll be following it up for the next two nights, you may be sure. After that, of course, I'll be a free agent in the matter."

Callender's eyes widened. "And what do you mean by that?"

"A pound a day isn't much, after all, and Mr. Newcastle might pay me better to keep his secrets to himself. He might even hire me to look into your affairs, especially the matter of a drab named Sally Wood."

"My God!" roared Callender. He swept his

walking stick across the table and sent bottle and glasses crashing to the floor. "I can't have everyone turn against me! What have I done to you?"

"Don't upset yourself, sir. It's only a matter of business. And you won't find a man in London who'll serve you more loyal or more honorable than Samuel Sayer. But just for the next two days, you understand. I have to live, too."

T E N

A Visitor from India

Reginald Callender sat in his uncle's study with the last bottle of his uncle's brandy on the desk in front of him. He still thought of what little was left in the house as his uncle's, since he himself had inherited nothing. And most of what had remained was gone now, sold to a furniture dealer to raise a bit of ready money. Callender had no head for business, just enough to know he had been cheated, but he hardly cared anymore. The laborers who came to loot the house had left him his bed and the trappings of this one room, where he had hidden while they gutted his birthright.

He had no idea what time it was. The thick velvet curtains kept out the sun, and he had already pawned his uncle's watch along with everything else pilfered from the coffin. His crime, if it had been one, had brought him discouragingly little. He poured another drink. The glass was dirty, and the bottle was dusty from its sleep in the cellar. He wondered how such things could be cleaned. This, along with such mysteries as the cooking of food or the washing of clothes, were as enigmatic to him as the secret of what lay beyond the grave. He had few skills. He could only smoke and swear, drink and dream, but even two of these required money he did not possess.

And his dreams, infuriatingly enough, were of Sally Wood. He cursed himself for this. Now, if ever, his self-interest demanded that he devote himself to dancing attendance upon Felicia Lamb, who clearly held his fate in her small hands. Yet it was Sally's heavy-lidded, full-lipped face that rose before him in the gloom, offering him not so much her beauty, and certainly not her love, but rather the sense of power that surged through him when he held her moaning in his arms. She could make him feel like a man again, and not the quivering, drink-soaked wretch he was becoming while he watched his fiancée and his fortune slip away. Still, to see her might be to risk everything: better to have another drink instead.

His trembling hand nearly dropped the

bottle when he heard a heavy pounding from somewhere in the house. He sat frozen in his chair, baffled and suspicious, until the sound came again and he realized it was someone knocking loudly on the front door. He attempted to ignore it, but the visitor was so insistent that Callender finally dragged himself to his unsteady feet and went out into the hall. Stripped of its furnishings, the empty house reminded him of Sebastian Newcastle's, and it was that scarred and sinister medium whom Callender half expected to greet on the doorstep.

Instead, there stood a stranger, a beefy, red-faced man with graying hair and clothing that was not only a decade out of fashion but seemed to have been cut to suit a man slimmer by several stone. He carried a small traveling bag in his left hand and looked ready to knock again with his right, when Callender pulled open the heavy oak door.

The two men peered at each other through a foggy gray that Callender dimly recognized as dusk, and at last the stranger spoke.

"Reggie?"

Callender, who was still at least sober enough to know his own name, did not find this an edifying remark.

"I know who I am, sir, damn your eyes, but who in blazes are you?"

"Don't you know me?"

"I've said as much, blast you! Go away!"

The man in the fog looked genuinely hurt. "But it's your cousin!" he said. "Nigel! Nigel Stone!"

Callender swayed in the doorway and blinked at his visitor. "Stone? From India?"

"That's right, and home at last. How's Uncle William?"

"Dead."

"Dead? Oh, dear. Sorry."

"Yes," said Callender. "You'd better come in."

Callender stepped unsteadily back inside. His cousin followed him into what Callender now realized was almost inpenetrable blackness. Nigel Stone paused for a minute, trying to get his bearings.

"My dear fellow! The place has been stripped bare!"

"Yes. Yes. It was the servants."

"Servants?"

"Yes. Servants. While I was at the funeral, they and their confederates stole all they could and carted it away."

"Good Lord. Beastly things, servants. Some of the brown fellows where I was would rob you blind if you didn't keep an eye on them. A blind eye, eh? Almost a joke."

"It's not funny to me, cousin."

"No. Of course not. Sorry."

"You'd better follow me into the study. This way."

The first thing Stone saw in the room was the brandy bottle flanked by two candles, stuck in their own grease to the surface of a massive desk. Callender sat down in a chair behind it and picked up his glass. In his haste to get his seat, he neglected the courtesy of offering one to his cousin.

"Tell me, Cousin Nigel, how is business in India?"

"Not so good, I'm afraid. That's why Uncle William summoned me."

"Oh? Just how bad is it?"

"Bloody damned bad, if you want to know, my dear fellow. Haven't a farthing."

"Nothing left at all?" asked Callender. His eyes glistened in the candlelight as he drained the glass.

"Oh, there's a few boxes of textiles that I had shipped back with me. They should be here in the morning, but that was all I could save. It took the last penny to pay my passage home. No. I'm a liar. I still have half a crown. See?"

"You idiot!" Callender leapt out of his chair and lunged across the desk. He grasped Stone by the collar and hauled him forward, snuffing out a candle and sending the bottle smashing

171

to the floor. Stone was too startled to do more than grunt at first, but when his cousin began to slam him against the desk, the older man broke free and pushed his drunken assailant across the room. Callender fell to the floor and lay there sobbing, both arms crossed over his face.

His cousin stood leaning on the desk, breathing heavily and wishing desperately for a drink from the broken bottle. "Empty anyway," he muttered. "Look here, Reggie! Are you all right?"

He moved hesitantly toward the quivering form on the carpet. "It wasn't my fault, really. It's conditions. You don't know what it's like there. Rebellion, robberies, and murder. The whole country's filled with madmen and fanatics. I was lucky to escape with my life!"

Callender sat up so suddenly that his cousin started back. "What is your life to me?" he wailed. "It's money that I need!"

"Really? What do you mean, old fellow? You must be rolling in the stuff. You're his heir, ain't you? I'm sure he didn't leave me anything, after all I've lost!"

Callender looked at Stone oddly. "What? His heir? Yes, of course I'm his heir." He laughed harshly. "But the money . . . the money isn't here yet. It's all tied up with those damned lawyers, and it may be weeks before I see any of it. You can see what a state I'm in."

"You really don't look well, my dear fellow," said Stone, helping Callender back to his chair. "I'm sorry to hear this, you know. Bit of trouble for both of us. I was really hoping, well, that I might be able to stay here for a while, just till I can get myself back on my feet, as it were . . . I can lend you half a crown . . ."

The two cousins laughed together, Stone with genuine mirth, Callender with a wheezing bitterness that ended with an offer of sorts. "I suppose you can stay, cousin, if you're willing to rough it."

"Rough it? I've done nothing else for ten years. We'll do fine together, eh? And buck up! It's only a matter of days."

"Days?" Callender asked sharply. "What day is this? What is the time?"

"Eh? It's Thursday, isn't it? And the last clock I passed said just after six, as near as I could see it through this damned fog."

"Thursday at six! Damn! I'm to dine with my fiancée in an hour."

"Your fiancée! Well, you are a fortunate fellow. And to think that I should find you in such a state." Stone paused and subjected his cousin to careful scrutiny. "You know, old fellow, you're really in no condition to meet a lady, or even a constable. You need a wash and a shave at least."

"Shave?" barked Callender. "With this hand? I might as well cut my throat and be done with it." The fingers he held before Stone's face were visibly trembling.

"I see. A case of the shakes. Well, we'll have to think of something else. I think I could do a bit of barbering, and I have a razor right here in my bag. You have some water? And a log for the fire. We must cheer you up, cuz. I mean to dance at your wedding."

"If there is a wedding."

"What? Something wrong?"

"Much. I'm half afraid I'm losing her. That damned spiritualist!"

"Eh? Someone out to lure her away from you? We can't have that."

"It hasn't come to that, I think," said Callender. "At least not yet. But he has some kind of hold on her, filling her head with stories of spooks, and spirits, and other worlds. I don't know how to fight it, but I feel he's changing her."

Nigel Stone's face was suddenly grimmer than Callender had imagined it could be. "That's a bad business," Stone said. "Very bad, fooling about with spirits."

"And what would you know about it?" sneered Callender.

"I didn't spend ten years in India for nothing, cuz. I may not have made any money, but at least I learned a thing or two. The whole country is rife with superstition, and what might be more than superstition. Men go mad believing in ghosts and demons there. They kill each other and they kill themselves, and some fall under spells that are unspeakable."

"Rubbish."

"I tell you it's not rubbish! These things can happen, cuz, and even if they don't, just thinking about them can do the worst sort of harm to body and soul. We must do something for this girl before it's too late."

"You do it, then," said Callender. "She only laughs at me when I try." He paused, and contemplated Stone with new interest. "You look like you could do with a good dinner."

"I could indeed."

"Then come along with me tonight, will you? See if you can scare this nonsense out of Felicia before it injures her. I always end up trapped with her accursed aunt anyway."

"Has she an aunt?"

"Yes, a spinster, and about your age, cousin, but don't even think of it. No man could bear her. You stick to the niece. And as for now, do you remember where Uncle William's wine cellar is?"

"Downstairs somewhere, isn't it?"

"That's the idea. Fetch us a bottle of port, will you? Then it will be soon enough for the fire, and the water, and the razor, don't you think?"

"As you say." Nigel Stone hesitated for a moment at the thought of the wine, since Callender clearly had no need of it, but he decided he could stand a drop himself, and that this was justification enough for a descent into the cellar. With one backward glance he started on his first task as the unpaid valet of the impoverished cousin he hoped would soon be a rich relative.

In the midst of what might have been a pleasant dinner, Stone tried to convince himself that the drop he had shared with his cousin really could not have made much difference. For Reginald Callender, helping himself to every decanter in sight, was as drunk as the lord he undoubtedly wished himself to be, and his increasingly erratic behavior interfered at least a bit with Stone's delight in the food, the drink, and the company.

Stone found the girl, Felicia Lamb, as pretty as a picture but not much more animated.

Her aunt Penelope, however, was a lively, birdlike little woman who not only kept his plate and his glass filled but had the courtesy if not the good taste to hang on his every word. For a man long cut off from polite society, such a dinner partner was a positive delight, and the luxury of the surroundings fulfilled the hopes that he had held for his uncle William's house. Stone grew expansive, but he also remembered his promise to his cousin.

"I understand you take an interest in spiritualism," he said to Felicia.

"I do," she replied evenly.

"Did it never occur to you that it might be dangerous?"

"Dangerous? You betray you kinship with Mr. Callender, sir. I refuse to accept the idea that my search for wisdom is a threat to me."

"No? You could be right, I suppose. I wouldn't want to contradict a lady, but some of the things I saw in India would be enough to make a man cautious. Or even a woman."

"Do tell us about it, Mr. Stone," purred Aunt Penelope. "I'm sure it's fascinating."

"Yes," interrupted Callender. "And informative, too. You listen to this, Felicia." His fiancée stiffened noticeably as he clumsily poured himself another brandy, spilling as much on the tablecloth as he did into his glass.

"Well," Stone began uncomfortably, "I don't want to make too much of this. Some of what goes on there is just tomfoolery, I reckon, like the fellows who send ropes into the air and then climb up 'em. No harm in that unless the rope breaks, eh?" He laughed, but only Aunt Penelope joined him. "I think it's just a trick anyway. What I mean to say is that some of 'em start out like that and then go on to do things that might hurt them badly. They think some of their gods or spirits are watching over them, so they feel free to walk on burning coals or lie down on beds of iron spikes. I've seen it! And they seem to be unharmed, too, but what if something went wrong, eh? What if the spirits weren't there when the fellow decided to take a nap? What then?"

"I'm sure I'm not interested in iron spikes, Mr. Stone," Felicia said.

"No, my dear young lady, I'm sure you're not. But neither were these chaps, once upon a time. Do you see what I'm driving at? Nobody's born thinking of such things; they're led into them by degrees."

"He's right, Felicia," said Callender. His speech was slurred, and she did not deign to reply.

"Then these things are really true?" asked Aunt Penelope.

"Damned if I know. Oh, pardon me. My point, though, is that it doesn't really matter if they're true or not, as long as people believe in 'em. Take the Thugs, for instance."

"Thugs?" asked Aunt Penelope. "Are they some sort of monster?"

"They're only men, but I suppose you could call 'em monsters, too. They're a cult of murderers—men, women, and children. Whole families of 'em, whole villages, maybe even whole cities, all mad from believing in the spirits of the dead and some goddess of the dead that wants them to kill. They prey on travelers. Wiped out a whole caravan I would have been on if I hadn't been ill, just as if the earth had swallowed 'em up. Lord Bentinck hanged a lot of these Thugs, I've heard, but there are more, you may be sure of it. That's what thinking too much about the dead can do!"

"I wish only to learn the secrets of the dead," said Felicia, "not to add to their number."

"The dead know nothing!" roared Callender. "Learn from me! Learn from life!"

"Really, Reginald," said Felicia coolly. "And shall I learn by example?"

"Example? And what is the example of the dead? Lie down and die yourself, I suppose?" Callender, drunk and angry, was halfway up from his seat, when Aunt Penelope tactfully interrupted.

"Please, Mr. Callender. Let us hear Mr. Stone out. And you be still, too, Felicia. It's not polite to argue with a guest, especially one who has traveled halfway around the world to give us the benefit of his experience. Do tell us more, Mr. Stone."

"Thank you, dear lady. What I mean to say is that if there are spirits, and you call them up, you can't tell what you'll get. If there are good spirits, there must be wicked ones, don't you think? In India, they tell tales of an evil spirit. It's called a baital, or a vetala, or some such thing. It gets into corpses somehow and makes them move about, and it draws the life out of every living thing it touches. Would you like to call up one of those? Could you put it down again?"

"It sounds like a vampire," Felicia suggested.

"Vampire? Oh, you mean that old book by Lord Byron. Read it when I was a lad. Quite made my hair stand on end. I suppose it's the same sort of thing."

"Please forgive me for contradicting you," said Felicia with excessive sweetness, "but *The Vampyre* was written by Lord Byron's physician, Dr. Polidori. I know a gentleman who met them both."

"Really? No doubt you're right. Not much of a literary man myself."

"She reads too much," mumbled Callender, but he was ignored.

"And take the ghouls," continued Stone.

"What?" demanded Callender.

"Ghouls. Not the kind we have here, not grave robbers exactly. The Indian ghouls are creatures who tear open graves and, well, feast on what they find there."

"How horrible." Aunt Penelope shuddered cheerfully.

"Isn't it? Of course we eat dead things ourselves, don't we? I hope the sheep who provided this excellent mutton has gone to its reward, eh?"

"Oh, Mr. Stone," laughed Aunt Penelope. "You're a wicked, wicked man."

"What's all this talk of robbing graves?" Reginald Callender was on his feet, a brimming glass of brandy in his hand. "You see what she does?" he shouted. "She turns us all into ghouls!" He whirled to face Felicia, and the brandy splashed over the front of her gown.

"Damn!" shouted Callender. He snatched up a napkin and applied it vigorously to her bodice.

"Your hands, sir!" cried Felicia.

"Mr. Callender!" gasped Aunt Penelope.

"My word!" said Nigel Stone.

Felicia Lamb jumped up and gathered her skirts around her. "I believe it's time that we were all in bed," she announced. Her ordinarily pale face was flushed a hot pink.

"Fine!" roared Callender. "Let's all go together!"

Felicia, her head held high, swept from the room. Callender laughed harshly and sank back into his chair, barely conscious of his surroundings.

"Oh, dear," said Aunt Penelope.

"Time to go home, old fellow," said Stone, pulling the comatose Callender to his feet. "My apologies, Miss Penelope. He took our uncle's death very hard."

"Good night, Mr. Stone. I hope you will call on us again."

"Nothing would please me more," said Stone, grunting under the weight of his burden as he backed toward the door. "Good night."

Almost before he knew it, Nigel Stone was in the street. He might as well have been at sea. The thick yellow fog made London look like a spirit world, one in which the misty glow of the street lamps revealed nothing but their own iridescence. His cousin was on his feet, but not much more. They had walked to dinner from Uncle William's house, and

Stone knew that it could not be far away, but he was a bit worse for the wine himself and was not really sure of his bearings.

He longed for a cab, and he wondered how lost he was. Callender said "Sally" several times, but this only confused his cousin more.

Helping Callender across an intersection, Nigel Stone heard a horse snorting, and he dragged his cousin back to a spot only a few feet from Felicia Lamb's house. Later, he convinced himself that he hadn't spoken to the driver because he realized they hadn't the money to hire a ride. What really decided him, though, before he even thought of his purse, was the sinister look of the driver. He was gaunt and pale, with dark hollows for eyes, and down the left side of his face ran a horrible scar.

ELEVEN

The Bride of Death

Felicia Lamb heard the old clock downstairs strike midnight before she thought it safe to rise from her curtained bed and begin to dress. It took her some time to prepare herself, but she was determined to do everything with exquisite care, for this was to be her ultimate rendezvous with the unknown.

She held neither lamp nor candle when she slowly pulled open the door of her bedchamber and slipped out into the dark hall, but she had lived in this house all her life and had no need of light to show her the way. Her only fear was what she might be detected, and that her aunt or the servants might try to protect her from what they might consider danger but which she had desired from the day of her birth. So that she could be sure of silence, her feet were bare.

She tiptoed quickly down the carpeted staircase, her hand resting heavily on the banister so that her tread would be light, then walked confidently through the hallway toward the door that led to the world outside. She felt for the bolt, moved it with a practiced hand, and opened the door. Yellow fog drifted in to meet her, and she stepped into its embrace. She pulled the iron key from her bosom and locked the house behind her so that all within it might be safe. Then she stepped out into the shrouded street, wrapping her hooded cloak around her.

The coach was where she was told it would be waiting. Neither she nor the driver spoke a word, and the hooves of horses had been muffled. There was hardly a sound to disturb the sleep of London as the coach rolled unerringly through the impenetrable mist.

Felicia still held the house key clutched tightly in her fingers, but when her conveyance had rounded several corners, she threw it into the gutter. It would never be recognized, and she did not intend to use it again.

She sat back quietly and waited to reach her destination, not even bothering to glance out the windows until the horses came to a smooth stop. She alighted without a moment's hesitation, then stood in thick clouds that might have been born in heaven or hell. A figure materialized beside her, almost as if it had drawn its substance from the fog; it guided her through a doorway and into darkness. Something shut behind her.

The two moved forward together, through a passageway that held at its end a globe of luminescence. Felicia felt that she was in a dream. The light resolved itself into a glowing ball of crystal, resting on an ebony table with chairs at either end, and casting its pale yellow glow on an all-encompassing shroud of black velvet curtains. She was in the consulting room of Sebastian Newcastle, and he stood at her side.

He moved away from her and seated himself at the far end of the table, his face aglow in sickly light. "Will you not remove your cloak and sit with me, Miss Lamb?

Felicia did neither. She was suddenly hesitant, suspicious. "Is this what you have promised me?" she said. "Only another séance?"

"Might it not be better so? There is much you could learn as you are, and much more that you may not wish to know."

"Then have you lied to me, sir?"

The light before Sebastian Newcastle's face flickered and dimmed. "Will you not wait, Felicia? What you seek comes soon enough, and lasts forever."

"Another séance, then? Will you call upon

the dead for me? Will you call the shade of anyone I name?"

"I shall do what I can."

"Then call for me the spirit of a wizard. A master of the darkness, one who mastered death and reckoned not the price. Call for me the spirit of your double, Don Sebastian de Villanueva. Can you do it, Mr. Sebastian Newcastle? Do you dare?"

"I can. But do you dare to let me?"

"Have I not asked it of you?"

"You have," he said. "You have asked too often to be denied. And yet the blame will be all mine."

"I absolve you," said Felicia Lamb.

"Spoken like the angel you so fervently desire to be," Sebastian said. His voice was almost brutal. "Will you do me the courtesy to sit down?"

"You can hardly hope to frighten me with gruff tones, when we have come so far," Felicia said.

"No. Nothing will frighten you but what you cannot change. And when that terror comes, will you be brave enough to bear it, or brave enough to put an end to it?"

"Surely I shall be one or the other," she replied as she seated herself at the table. "Shall we begin?"

"I warn you because I care for you," Sebastian said.

"I believe it," she said. "Now show me who it is that cares for me so much."

She reached out for his cold hand, but he drew back. He did not speak. He crossed his arms before his face, and the light in the crystal was snuffed out in an instant. The black room was entombed in ebony.

Felicia stared ahead, her hand at her heart, more frightened than she would have admitted under torture. Something was about to happen, something she had longed for, but she was half afraid that she would be ravished and murdered in the dark. Was that what she had demanded?

She hoped for a vision, but instead she heard a voice. It might have been human, indeed it must have been human, but the low, echoing, senseless syllables sounded more like an animal in agony. It ended in a note that was a hollow song of pain.

Sebastian's face appeared abruptly in the gloom. His flesh glowed with the pale blue light of putrescence, and the flame of decay grew brighter, until the features burned away and left only a gleaming silver skull beneath. It spoke to her.

"What is worse than death, my love? Flee from it!"

The skull's mouth was full of unnaturally sharp teeth that gleamed like swords. The skull screamed and then burst into flame. A dull and rusted blade dropped from the ceiling and sundered the skull from whatever held it erect. The flashes of fire turned cold blue as it rolled across the table toward Felicia; the hollow sockets where its eyes had been bubbled with globes of glistening jelly, while locks of black, silky hair sprouted from the burnished surface of the silver skull.

The head fell upon her breast, and all at once Sebastian was in her arms. The black room was alive with silver.

"I am the one you seek," he told her. "Turn away."

Felicia pulled away from him and stood, leaving him on his knees, his head bent over the arms of the ebony chair. He turned toward her, relieved to think that she would run from all that he could offer. She took a deep breath, then pulled the dark hood from her face and the dark cloak from her body.

"I am the one you seek," she said. "Would you deny my desire, and your own?"

She wore a white wedding gown, its silk scarcely paler than her own ivory flesh.

The gown had been her mother's, forty years ago, when fashion was more graceful and less refined. Her arms were bare, her shoulders were bare, and her breasts were almost bare as well, the silk gathered beneath them and flowing down in delicate folds that brushed against the ebony floor. Felicia would never have dared to dress in such a manner if it had not been her wedding night, but now she exulted in her shamelessness. The glow around her turned the silk, her skin, her pale eyes, and her ashen hair to silver.

The black figure of Sebastian Newcastle glided toward her.

"Destiny," he murmured.

He grasped her almost cruelly. She felt his cold breath upon her throat, his cold fingers in her flowing hair. She arched her back and exposed her white neck, but Sebastian pulled her forward and turned away from her.

He would not look at her as he spoke.

"I have become what I am, a creature of the night who feeds on blood, because I would not die. Why should you, a young woman with years of life before her, spurn the most precious gift in all creation?"

"Because I would know more of its creator." She reached out to touch his shoulder.

"If you care nothing for yourself, think of your friends. Think of your family."

"I have no friends," Felicia said. "As for my family, those I love most have gone before me. As for Aunt Penelope, I think she will be content with my fortune."

"And the young man?"

"You have seen what he is. I wish to God that I had seen it sooner."

"Then is there nothing for you in this world?"

"Nothing but to be rid of it."

"Then at least die a true death," Sebastian said, "and I will guide your spirit as I do those others you have seen, those who are lost. Take poison, cut your throat, jump from a tower, do anything but take this curse upon yourself. For many centuries I have carried it alone, and it is better so."

"You have not renounced your fate. In truth, I think you relish it. You love to be a lord of life and death, to stand between them and cast a cold eye on both. Is it because I am a woman that you think I do not know my own desires? Do you think that I am not as brave as you? Could it not be that I have been sent to end your loneliness forever?"

Sebastian whirled to confront her, his face a mask of fury. "Loneliness? Why need I be lonely when I have companions such as this to comfort me?"

The glowing curtains rippled in the black and silver room behind Sebastian. A shape appeared behind them: aimless, clumsy, menacing, and unutterably sad. A faltering white hand emerged through the drapes, and despite herself Felicia gasped. What shuffled into the room had once been a boy. His shaggy hair was red, but his slack-jawed face was almost gray, and his eyes were those of an idiot. His lips were drooling, and his teeth were sharp. He limped toward Sebastian, one leg twisted and broken.

"Please, sir," he muttered.

"My God, Sebastian," Felicia said. "What is this?"

"A grave robber. He said his name was Henry Donahue. I found him and another at their work, and killed the first one outright, but by the time I caught young Donahue again, my fury and my bloodlust were so great that I slaked my thirst on him. And here he is, one of the living dead, and quite mad. I should have destroyed him, and surely I must, but now I am happy to have been delayed. Gaze on him. Is this what you wish to become?"

At the sound of her voice the dead boy had turned toward Felicia. He dragged his shattered leg across the black carpet, his eyes fastened on her throat. Felicia felt suddenly naked and defenseless.

"Please, miss," said the boy.

He touched her.

Suddenly his hands were reaching for her throat, his dirty little teeth gnashing at the air as she tried to push him away. There was a strange strength in his small fingers. Felicia screamed.

The boy had her half sprawled on the ebony table, when Sebastian yanked him back by his red hair and threw him across the room. Half of his scalp stayed in Sebastian's hand, and his head was a raw but bloodless wound as he implacably scuttled over the floor to reach the woman he wanted.

Sebastian pounced on him again, caught his twisted leg, and dragged the snarling creature through the velvet curtains and out of the room.

Felicia was alone, her heart pounding, her breath coming in frantic gasps. She was terrified, and yet exhilarated, too. She struggled down from the tabletop and collapsed into an ebony chair. From somewhere in the recesses of the house came a high-pitched wail of agony that rose to a crescendo and then stopped abruptly. Felicia knew she would never see the boy again.

She waited.

When Sebastian returned to her, his hair hung over his face and his clothes were torn. His hands were spotted with blood. He looked at them and then at Felicia.

"There was little enough in him," Sebastian said. "He had been starved. Now you see what I would save you from."

Felicia trembled, but she remained where

she was. "Between you and this boy is as much difference as there must have been in life," she said. "I will not be like him."

"Go!" shouted Sebastian, but even as he did he advanced upon her, his mouth twisting uncontrollably.

Felicia gritted her teeth and clutched the arms of the ebony chair with all her might. She held her head high and felt the pulses throbbing in her long white neck as Sebastian overwhelmed her.

Then they were on the carpet, her carefully coiffed pale hair spilled upon its darkness, her gown in disarray, her body throbbing with delight and dread. She felt an ecstasy of fear, stunned more by the desires of her flesh than by the small, sweet sting she felt as he sank into her and life flowed between them. She rocked and moaned beneath the body of the man she loved. She took life and love and death and made them one.

And when it was over, Sebastian arose alone. She lay at ease, her limbs sprawled in a graceful carelessness, her face marked by an abandon hardly tinged by shock. She was pale as a marble statue, colored with a few fresh drops of virgin's blood. She was at peace, but Sebastian knew that she would rise full of dark desire when the next sun set.

His tears, when they came, were tinged with her bright blood.

TWELVE

Blood Money

Samuel Sayer's five nights of servitude were over, and now his real work could begin. It was a point of honor with him never to turn on a client who was still paying him, but Mr. Reginald Callender's five pounds had bought all the time they could, and now the detective could call himself a free agent once again. Evidently his attempts to alternately discourage and frighten the young man had been successful; either that or the poor fool had been unable to raise any more cash. Sayer would send him a note in the morning formally resigning from the case, but meanwhile there was more important business to be conducted.

From the shadow of a tall cedar Sayer had

an unobstructed view of the entrance to Sebastian Newcastle's house. He had watched men and women come and go throughout the evening, but the last of them had departed almost an hour ago, and now it was Sayer's turn to pay a visit. He reassured himself by feeling in his pocket for his pistol, its soft lead ball rammed into place by his own strong hand. There might be more modern weapons, with better accuracy at a longer range, but the detective knew from experience just how much devastation that large hot lump of malleable metal could inflict as it tore through a man's insides. No opponent was powerful enough to stand against it. He had even carved a cross on the ball to make sure that it would shatter at the moment of impact, and he was confident that nothing on earth could survive the single shot.

Yet he felt a vague twinge of apprehension as he stepped stealthily from behind his tree and moved onto the path that led toward the spiritualist's house. A plain house of plain brick was nothing to be frightened of, surely, even if the dim lights in two upstairs windows created the impression that huge flat eyes were watching him, but Sayer knew just enough about Sebastian Newcastle to suspect that he might be a dangerous man—not just a thieving, murderous brute, but a villain rich in tricks and treachery. Some risk was always involved in meeting such a man on his own ground, but Samuel Sayer was not without stratagems himself, and if all went well, he would leave this place much wealthier than when he arrived.

As he approached the house, moving with the silence that had become almost an instinct with him, Sayer kept his eyes on those two lighted windows looming over him. They were far enough apart to encompass the entire second story, and surely were part of two separate rooms. He was wondering what might be going on in those two rooms, when suddenly both lights went out at once.

Sayer froze, his hand extended to pull the bell chain he had noticed other visitors employing. His mind told him that what had happened was due to no more than some sort of conjurer's device, perhaps nothing more complex than the timed work of two confederates, though he had been almost sure Newcastle was alone in the house. But whatever his mind said, the detective's heart had given a tremendous thump such as he had never felt while tracking down a cutpurse or a cutthroat.

He took several deep breaths to pull himself together and reached for the bell chain again, but before he had a chance to touch it, the white wooden door in front of him began to open slowly and silently. Sayer immediately reached for his pistol, then realized that he would be showing his hand as well as his weapon and tried to remain calm. He would see who was behind the door soon enough.

And yet, when it was opened so wide that he heard it brush against the adjoining wall, there was no one in sight. Ahead of Sayer was an empty coal-black corridor, so dark that it might have been one of the pits of hell. A heavy thump echoed from somewhere in the recesses of the building.

"Is anybody there?" croaked the detective. His voice sounded weak even to him; he cleared his throat and tried again. "I have an appointment," he went on, his voice stronger but still hollow in the empty hall. "I've come about . . ." What had he come about? "The spirits," he finally whispered.

There was no reply.

Sayer waited. He peered into the darkness. He took a step forward. "I'm coming in," he started to say but choked on the words; he sounded like a fool. Every nerve in his body was screaming for him to retreat, but he took another step, and then another.

And as soon as he was well into the black hallway, the heavy door slammed shut behind him and he was lost in darkness.

Sayer cursed himself for jumping at the sound. He had been expecting it, but somehow that did nothing to detract from the shock he felt. He was a trapped animal; he might as well have been a blind one, too.

A carpet seemed to lie beneath his feet, but it was all that he could feel, and when he stretched out a hand, he quickly drew it back again as if he feared what it might encounter in the dark.

Instead, he moved backward, his fingers groping for the door that was his only point of reference. With that at his back, he would at least be safe from attack in one direction. He almost lost his balance when his searching hands met no resistance, yet even staggering back brought him no closer to his goal. When two more paces left him still adrift, he decided that he must have somehow turned around. This hardly seemed possible, but there was no other explanation. He began to move in large circles, but still his outstretched arms touched nothing. Considering the dimensions of the corridor, this was patently impossible. Sayer knew he was the victim of some sort of trick but felt panic rising in him anyway, especially when he heard another loud thump to his left.

He started away from the sound, but it was followed by another, and then one more, each closer and each noisier. The floor shook beneath his feet as if a stone colossus were bearing down on him, and the detective let out a low moan that was lost in the next resounding crash. Sayer was on one knee, hands groping frantically; the carpet seemed to buckle and sway below him. His pistol was forgotten, his hat was lost, his clothes in disarray.

He would have been screaming in an instant if the light had not appeared, coming so unexpectedly that he was virtually struck dumb.

Perhaps it was just as well. For there he was, groveling on the carpet just inches from the door, while over him stood the black-clad figure of Sebastian Newcastle, a silver candlestick held aloft in each of his long, pale hands.

"You are late, Mr. Sayer," he said quietly. "In fact, I expected you some nights ago. You might as well have come in then, you know. It could hardly have been comfortable for you, waiting outside in the cold and damp, but now, I see, you have made yourself at home."

"So you know me," Sayer observed, drawing himself up from the floor with all the dignity that he could muster. He glanced around but saw only the narrow hallway as it had been before, empty save for the presence of his host.

"I have known you for many years. The last

time our paths crossed, however, you were wise enough to turn away."

"I don't know what you're talking about. I came here for a consultation, and I sent a letter asking for an appointment."

"Using a false name. Surely we know each other better than that?"

"Perhaps you're right at that," Sayer acknowledged. "I've always had my best success when all parties laid their cards on the table."

"You wish me to read the cards for you?"

"No need to be funny, Mr. Newcastle, even if you did make a fool of me just now. The place must be full of machinery, just like Mr. Callender said."

"Are you a friend of Mr. Callender?"

"Not anymore I'm not, but I'd be willing to bet you know all about that. You're a deep one, aren't you? Anyway, the business I have in mind would be strictly between you and me, and beneficial to us both. One of the benefits would be to rid you of Callender."

"I see," Newcastle said. "You mean you are prepared to kill him for me?"

"I hardly think it needs to come to that," Sayer stammered. He realized with some discomfort that Newcastle had not moved since his unexpected appearance and was still standing at the end of the corridor like a black statue. "Look here! Is there somewhere we can sit and talk?"

"I beg your pardon, Mr. Sayer. I see you are uncomfortable. Follow me, please, and I will find you a chair and some refreshment."

Newcastle's eyes were dark and dull even in the glimmer of the twin flames he carried, and his long mustache hid any expression that might have been visible on his thin lips. Sayer was hardly eager to follow the man who wore that impassive mask into his lair, but that was the task he had set for himself, and it would be unforgivable to back out now. Those moments in the corridor might have been unnerving, but they might also have made the spiritualist overconfident, and that could work to Sayer's ultimate advantage. Not chancing it would mean an ignominious retreat, and another of Sebastian Newcastle's sneers.

Sayer followed the retreating figure down the corridor to the double doors at the end and tried to betray no surprise when they opened with no sign of human aid. At Newcastle's gesture, Sayer preceded his host into the black room.

"The machinery you have installed in this house must have set you back a fortune," he observed as the doors closed behind them. "It would be a pity if you were obliged to move."

"Machinery?" echoed Newcastle. "Then you do not believe in the supernatural?"

"I believe in what I can see, in what I can touch."

"Then at least you believe in the floor outside. I hope that it was not too dusty for you." Newcastle glided past his guest to stand behind a round table flanked by two tall ebony chairs. "Take a seat," Newcastle said. "I promise that it will be equally convincing."

Sayer did as he was told, perching uncomfortably on edge of the wooden slab beneath him as he looked around the room. Everything was black: the floor, the ceiling, the curtains that covered the walls. The medium's clothes were black, too, and his flesh was the dead white of an invalid's, though he seemed strong enough. The detective could see no color anywhere except for the two yellow flames atop the candles that Newcastle placed on the table, and then there was a flash of red before his face.

It was a bottle of wine.

Newcastle settled it between the silver candlesticks as he sat down, and all at once his hands held silver goblets encrusted with what might have been real jewels. Sayer could not see where all of this had come from but reasoned that there was ample room for everything beneath the medium's long coat. This was no more than a bit of stagecraft.

"These are very old," the spiritualist said,

running the sharp nail of his index finger around the rim of the goblet closest to hand, "and so is the wine."

He uncorked the bottle with disturbing ease and tipped it toward the detective's goblet, but Sayer covered the flow with his hand. A small splash of the sticky liquid dribbled over him, and he reached for his handkerchief to clean himself.

"I don't care much for wine," he said.

"Perhaps you think there's poison in it." Newcastle almost seemed to be smiling.

"There could be, or drugs at least. A touch of opium, to give your victims visions."

Newcastle silently poured himself half of the bottle and drank it down at once. A drop of red trickled down his pale chin. "You can see how wholesome it really is," he said.

"Some of your kind thrive on it," Sayer replied, "but I prefer my own tipple, if you won't take it amiss." He reached into his own coat, of an honest navy blue that still looked black in this dim light, and pulled out a small flask. "This is silver, too," he said with a touch of pride. He took a pull on the flask, and then another.

"Something to warm a man on a cold night," Newcastle said. "Peach brandy."

Sayer stared at him with an expression close to awe. "Surely you didn't try to find out even that," he said. "You're quite a thorough investigator!"

"I can smell it," Newcastle told him. "My senses are unusually acute."

"I see." The detective felt warmth coursing through his system, and it made him bold. He put the flask back into one pocket and recalled what he had in the other pocket that was even more comforting. "Then no doubt you can tell me why I came to see you?"

"To speak to the spirits, certainly. What other reason could there be?" Newcastle spoke calmly, rationally, as though their exchange were no more than the business of ordinary life, but when he stopped speaking, his tongue flicked out to catch the line of red liquid on his chin, and it seemed to be unnaturally, horrifyingly long.

Sayer blinked, and shook his head, and when he looked again, there was nothing out of the ordinary to be seen. Yet now he was almost certain that Sebastian Newcastle was smiling.

"Forgive me if I joke with you," Newcastle said. "I understand you have no wish to speak to the dead, although not all wishes are fulfilled. And I know that you have come here for money. Blood money, I believe it's called."

"Blood money," muttered Sayer. "Yes, that's what they called it. An honest Bow

Street runner brings a man to justice; he is rewarded for his work; and if the prisoner is executed, then people say we've taken blood money. It's as if we were murderers ourselves, and not the ones who battled them."

"So you have not been loved, Samuel Sayer. And you would have been loved less if people knew how many times the gold you took came from criminals who wished to go about their business undetected. That was blood money for a certainty, and that is what you expect to get from me tonight."

"Well, what of it?" the detective spluttered. "I have to live, don't I? After all, I'm only human."

"Your continued existence may not seem as imperative to others as it does to you," observed Newcastle. "And the argument that you are human has little weight to one who has seen what the human race can do."

The medium's voice was quiet and conversational, but its very remoteness disturbed Sayer in a way that no mere bluster could have achieved. Nonetheless he lounged back in his chair and reached for his silver flask. "You'll pay," he said before he drank. "My silence is cheap compared to the alternative."

Newcastle leaned forward and rested his arms on the ebony table. His face, thrust forward, was uncomfortably close to Sayer's own. "And what have you to tell, that I should pay blood money to keep it secret?"

"That you are a fraud. That you prey on helpless women. And that you have designs on the fortune of a Miss Felicia Lamb."

"I see. And your witness is Reginald Callender?"

"No. I hardly need him now, with what I know. My offer is to keep your business safe from him."

"You know nothing," said Newcastle. "But you might be inconvenient. How much gold would it take to still your tongue? Would this be enough?"

A bulging leather pouch was in Newcastle's hand, and then its contents were spilling out upon the tabletop. Dozens of thick gold coins rattled and came to rest, their surfaces gleaming richly in the candlelight as they piled up around the deep red of the medium's wine bottle.

Sayer had a fortune in his grasp, but he resisted the temptation to snatch it up at once. Instead, he selected the single coin that had rolled closest to him and held it to the light. He had never seen its like before. No British mint had manufactured it, but the pressure of his teeth assured him that it was no counterfeit.

Sayer put the coin back on the black table.

"Yes, I think this would do nicely," he finally said. "In fact, I might say your generosity overwhelms me. But somehow I don't think you mean to let me get away with all this gold."

"What is there to prevent you?"

"Just what you said before, about me and the men you say I shielded. I didn't like the sound of that. It sounded like you knew something. Almost like a warning."

"Then you think we are two of a kind, do you, Mr. Sayer? You think I mean to blackmail you? I assure you that I want none of your money. My needs are modest."

Sayer's blue eyes were cold. "There's no evidence against me, anyway. I'm not such a fool as that. I believe you're bluffing me, Mr. Newcastle."

"And I believe the same of you. I admit, however, it might prove inconvenient if you tried to bring the police here. And that's also the only thing that might put you at risk, Mr. Sayer. If I were called upon to prove that I could truly summon up the spirits of the dead, I might beckon to some of your old friends. They're my friends now, the dead, but you might find them an embarrassment. This man, for example!"

Sayer squirmed in his seat and glanced back at the door behind him as if he half expected to see someone entering, but the visitor Newcastle had announced chose a different means of making his presence felt. As Sayer stared intently, he saw the medium's face in front of him begin to change. The cheeks swelled, the features coarsened, the thickening nose twisted as if it had been broken more than once, and in a few more seconds Sayer was gazing into the brutish eyes of a man he had never expected to see again.

The reunion was not to his liking. He saw hatred in that fiercely impatient face, and he was cringing from the force of it, when all at once there was no one else in the room with him but the spiritualist called Sebastian Newcastle.

"I see you recognized the man," he said. "Would you care to hear his voice? Or the voices of the victims he claimed while you protected him from justice?"

"I've heard enough," snarled Sayer.

"The dead speak with many tongues, you know, and not always with the tongues of angels. There are thousands of them all around us now in this great field called All Souls. They are my flock. My congregation. And my will is their desire."

The medium's voice was rising with the passion of an inspired preacher, and the darkness around his head grew misty with strange

211

wisps of yellow fog. Dim faces floated in the air, and a keening choir of the dead seemed to raise a litany from somewhere in the earth. The figure of the medium grew larger than any man should be, so vast that for a moment the detective did not even see the fingers that reached out for him across the tabletop.

The fingers stretched out toward Sayer like uncoiling snakes; they were monstrously long, and they were utterly obscene.

Sayer sat frozen for an instant, but before the thing that had been Newcastle got a grip on him, a Bow Street runner's reflexes brought the pistol out of his coat pocket. Then the grotesque fingers were upon him, while over him soared a hideous countenance whose gaping mouth flashed with silver fangs that dripped dark wine. The dead wailed all around.

Sayer felt a cold grip on his good right hand and felt the small bones crack, but still he had the fortitude to jerk the barrel of his pistol up and fire at point-blank range into the face that loomed above him.

The report reverberated through the black room like a clap of thunder signaling the day of judgment, and in the flash of the gunpowder Sayer saw a huge red hole rip through Newcastle's face.

The detective pulled away and let his adversary fall facedown among the golden coins. The room was deathly still; the spirits, or whatever they had been, were gone. There was only candlelight, a corpse, and the pungent odor of gunsmoke. That, and a small fortune in gold.

Sayer examined his right hand, releasing his grip on the pistol as carefully as he could, but still not without a wince. There were broken bones, no doubt of it, but he'd had worse. He moved forward to look at the body slumped in front of him, and blessed the caution that had caused him to carve a deep cross on his ball of lead. It had clearly shattered on impact, as he had intended, and the back of Newcastle's skull was no more than a jagged hollow gleaming with brains and blood. Neither man nor devil could have survived such a wound.

Sayer cast his eye around while he listened intently for any sign of life inside the house. There was nothing.

"It's as I said," he murmured. "Machines, or drugs, or hypnotism. Whatever it was, it's gone where you've gone, Mr. Sebastian Newcastle. Still, I'll admit you gave me quite a turn. And to make up for that, you'll give me all this lovely money."

The detective in Sayer urged him to stay for at least a few minutes, seeking out the secrets that had made Newcastle seem so formidable.

Such things would certainly be worth knowing, but there was also the matter of murder and the chance that someone might have heard the shot. The old Bow Street runner would have to be content with a more tangible reward.

He noted with some distaste that most of the coins scattered over the table had been splashed with the spiritualist's blood, which was rapidly forming a puddle from which each separate piece of gold would have to be plucked. Sayer was hardly squeamish, but bloodstains were evidence. Pocketing the money would necessitate burning his coat at the first opportunity, though it was some consolation to realize that he would certainly be able to buy a new one.

His mind was running through the list of fences who might be equipped to handle such strange currency, while his fingers reached out for the first coin. He cursed as it slipped through his fingers: He had forgotten about the injury to his right hand. His fingers were stained red, of course, but even in the dim light from the candles he saw that his thumb had been deeply cut. A rich gout swelled from the wound, and Sayer realized that the coins had sharp edges.

He would have to be more careful, and he would have to hurry, too.

Sayer squatted on his haunches as he

snatched one of the silver candlesticks from the tabletop, using his good hand for the job because he had no choice. He squinted as he thrust his head under the table and spied the elusive gold piece almost at once. He leaned forward, nearly lying on the floor, and his broken, bleeding hand had almost grasped its prize when a dribble of gore from the edge of the table caught him in the eye.

"Bloody hell," said Samuel Sayer as his hand clutched convulsively, knocking the coin aside.

The gold disc skittered away from him and rolled across the carpet into a dark corner. He decided to let it lie. Time was of the essence. Wiping his eyes, he crawled out of the darkness and placed the candlestick where it had been. With his left hand he reached out for another slippery coin, and he might have held on to it if he had not chosen this moment to look up.

The corpse of Sebastian Newcastle was erect in its chair, its bloody face leering at him.

Shock caused Sayer to lose his grip, and a gleaming bit of gold and red shot out from between his fingers with such force that it careened off a wall before it was lost in shadows.

Sayer hardly knew what to think. Had he moved the corpse? He was certain he had not, but what other explanation could there be? Evidently the spiritualist's tricks had disturbed him more than he was willing to admit, but none of that mattered now. Sayer's task was simply to collect his money and be gone.

He took a firm step toward the table, arm outstretched, and slipped in a puddle of blood.

He crashed into the table, jolting Newcastle's body into a hideous parody of life, while dozens of the dripping coins went scattering and rattling to the floor. And he was cut again.

He stared at Newcastle's blasted features in fear and fury, still taking time to notice that the wound there seemed less severe than what he had recalled. Still, it had been the back of the head that had borne the full force of the expanding lead. But there was something else wrong here.

The coins were still dancing around the carpet; he could hear the sound they made long after he knew it should have ceased. One of them leapt up from the floor and flew with deadly speed past his head.

This was, of course, impossible, but Sayer felt a wet warmth spreading down his neck and saw something pink drop down upon the table.

It was the top half of his ear.

Gleaming bits of gold flew from the table and rang in ricochet around the rooms. They sang like bullets. One of them ripped through Samuel Sayer's already brutalized right hand, and he knew that he would never use it again, but that was the least of his worries.

He tried to dodge the deadly hail, but if was as if he were being fired upon by an entire regiment. A bit of metal that might have supported him for months smashed into his kneecap and sent him crashing to the ground. Another golden coin ripped through his throat.

Sayer's blood was splashing everywhere. Through the dim haze of his fading sight, behind the glistening hail of gold, he could barely make out the figure of Sebastian Newcastle, his face incredibly healing itself, rising from the chair where he had died.

"Blood money," said Newcastle, and Samuel Sayer knew no more.

Sebastian looked down at the dying man. He had not been bitten, and thus was not infected, but still there was a use for his blood, rapidly leaking away, and this was no time to consider the source. Sebastian snatched up the two silver goblets, rushed across the room, and held them to Samuel Sayer's gushing throat. He gathered all he could, then scooped up the remnants from the carpet in his bare hands and licked them clean.

One cup he drained, but the other he kept for Felicia, whom he would soon awaken.

Before he slept, Newcastle knew that he must write to Callender in Samuel Sayer's hand, explaining that there was nothing amiss in the house by the cemetery, that the boy who lurked outside was no more than a servant, that Mr. Newcastle was above reproach, and that the former Bow Street runner was abandoning the case.

Perhaps this should be done first, in fact. Then there would be time enough to initiate Felicia Lamb into the world that she had chosen when she wished to become a vampire.

Sebastian's head still throbbed, and he wondered idly what the cross on the bullet might have done to him if it had not shattered when it struck his skull. Sayer had been just a bit too clever.

Sebastian looked around the room and realized how ghastly it might seem to a new initiate. He would have to clean house before he did anything else.

His thoughts were troubled. Callender could be dealt with, certainly, but he feared for Felicia.

T H I R T E E N

Thirst

Felicia drifted through darkness. It seemed to her that she was in a dream, hovering between sweet sleep and an awakening that might be sweeter still, yet she was content to wait for what might come, floating on a sea of silence until she reached its shore. A yearning welled up within her, a longing such as she had never known before, but the desire was as pleasing to her as the dream, and almost a rapture in itself. Felicia felt that she could lie in this slumber forever, and did not doubt that such a future might be hers until she heard the sound of footsteps close at hand.

She stirred luxuriously, wondering only dimly what messenger had come to summon her, and still less what that summons might entail, when her shoulder brushed against a surface that was cold and hard. This hardly startled her, and puzzled her not at all, but its touch on her cool skin seemed nothing like the caress of the deep ocean that had carried her, and nothing like the comfort of the feather-bed in which she knew she would awake.

Strangely enough, it seemed more like a box.

Memory began to seep into her mind, of a rapture tinged with an unholy fear. As the footsteps approached, she realized finally who it must be, but more than that, she understood what had become of her. She knew she had been drifting through the realm that bordered death and that she had returned to a new world, utterly alien, where those who still lived claimed to hold dominion.

Panic rushed up to enfold her, less at the thought of what she was than at the fear of what she might soon be, and then Sebastian opened her coffin.

He frightened her more and less than he ever had before. She wanted nothing more than to sink back into the darkness that had soothed her, and yet his eyes drew her up toward him and the London of the living, even if he was no more alive than she.

There was something in his eyes now that she had never seen. The dark, enigmatic hollows that had tempted her like an abyss now sparkled with brilliant lights like a sky full of shooting stars, and the flesh that had seemed so pale now glowed with an unearthly luminescence. He looked to her like some sort of dark angel, and she knew that the transformation had been not in him but in her perception. She was the one who had been changed.

Sebastian, beholding her white radiance, gathered Felicia Lamb into his arms. She had no idea where she was, but the garish flare of their embrace showed her a shadowy vault of stone and another coffin, trimmed with silver, that lay beside her own. Her eyes were flooded with cold fire, yet nothing shone as brightly as the silver, jewel-encrusted goblet that Sebastian offered her.

"Drink," he said.

She reached out for the silver cup, touched it, and then turned away. She wondered was in it. She knew.

"Drink," Sebastian implored her.

She took the brimming cup in both her hands and stared into its depths; it seemed to be filled with fire. The red glow was warmth and power. It was love. She tried to raise it to her lips, but her fingers trembled uncontrollably; she swayed, upright in her coffin.

Was this a test? Was it a temptation or a triumph? She could not hold the goblet. It crashed to the floor.

The ruddy liquid pulsed for a moment on

the surface of the flagstones, then seeped between the cracks into the earth and disappeared. Sebastian's fingers reached for it, his knees bent toward it, but he rose again. The empty goblet rolled across the floor.

Felicia scurried after the silver cup and captured it. She squatted on the floor and gazed at the empty goblet as if it might be a symbol full of mysteries. When she looked up at Sebastian, he had turned away from her.

"Blood," she said. "You offered me human blood."

The gleaming face with its jeweled eyes turned toward her once again. "It is our destiny," Sebastian said quietly. "You knew as much when you offered yourself to me."

"But there was more I did not know. As I am now, I realize what it means to take another's life, to be the cause of death."

"It means nothing," Sebastian replied. "Their lives end in one way or another. They are no more than cattle to our kind."

Felicia lifted her eyes to his, and he saw the cold light glistening in them. "It is too late for you to lie to me," she said, "now that I see so much of what you were afraid to show me. This is why you resisted for so long, because you knew what it meant to be transformed into a predator."

"And is that what you would call me now?"

"It is what I call myself," she said.

Their eyes met like mirrors, showing all and showing nothing in the same glance. "You are young in the ways of this new world," Sebastian said. "Trust me for a little while, and all will become clear to you."

He took her hand and led her toward a doorway, and through it to a flight of stairs that led upward from the darkness of the earth into the darkness of the night. Then they were in a passageway, one which Felicia recognized. She turned instinctively toward the black room.

"Not there," Sebastian said. "Not now."

"The one you killed is there," Felicia said. "The one whose blood you offered me."

"He was an enemy."

Felicia glided away from the closed door of the black room. "I had no enemies till now," she said.

"None that you knew," Sebastian replied.

He led her out under the night sky, and she was dazzled by the starry wonder of it. The light from each distant sun streamed like a banner toward the earth in colors of gold and green, crimson, and cobalt. The world was a vision in which only her guide seemed absolutely real; even the bulky brick house behind her seemed no more than a hallucination, a flickering dream devoid of weight, stability, or permanence. Only light and spirit were genuine; all else was illusion. Felicia felt like an awestruck child.

She stroked Sebastian's glowing face. "I remember you," she said, "from years ago. You rescued me. You spared me. That was you. Of course."

"Would that I had spared you once again," Sebastian said.

"My life was yours before I even knew what life could be. A dream of flying, and leaving everything behind. This is wonderful, Sebastian."

"There are more wonders than these. Every power that I have exhibited to you is yours, if you will give me time. What is a life that is destined to be lost in any case compared to this?"

His glowing flesh seemed to pulsate with an inner flame, and to flicker as a fire might; then it dispersed like smoke. Sebastian had become a radiant mist, vanishing into the night fog, but still Felicia sensed his presence reaching out to her as a voice that made no sound spoke to her, with an authority that could not be denied.

The voice urged her to join it, to become part of the darkness, and her unspoken answer was that this was, of course, impossible, yet still Sebastian pressed on, denying her denial, until she felt a power rise within her that burst the shackles of the flesh and set her free into the realm of pure spirit.

Nothing in her life had prepared her for such absolute exhilaration. To know, as she had always hoped to know, that there was life beyond the body meant little compared to the delight she felt in the experience itself. She was a ghost, a goddess, a free soul, yet she was still herself, free of all restraint, free of all earthly bonds, but still Felicia Lamb.

And when the misty glow she had become flowed into the fog that was her lover, Felicia was on fire.

Sebastian had possessed her physically, taking her life and her love in one stroke, and that had been ecstasy, but it had been only a symbol, a faint shadow of the commingling of kindred souls that now was theirs. Everything of man's creation or man's desire dropped away: the streets, the city, and the earth itself. What was left was only passion and release. It was a kind of joyous music.

Or so it seemed at first, for there was also sorrow. The sorrow emanated from Sebastian, and at first it sounded as no more than a high, thin note in the resounding chord, but gradually the discord grew into a scream, a wail so penetrating that it clotted mist and light and fog as if they were blood. Felicia found herself in the arms of a gaunt man whose eyes were duller than jewels and whose flesh was dimmer than moonlight.

"If there were only the dream," Sebastian said, "then we would not be damned."

Felicia froze. She was waltzing with a corpse, and she was one herself. She was consumed by a terrible thirst.

Sebastian knew her need at once, as well as any creature could, and he wondered how soon the craving would conquer her. He wanted to postpone the moment for as long as he could because he knew that she might turn from the temptation when she saw it.

He needed more time.

He took her by the hand and hurried her across the way toward Kensal Green, toward All Souls Cemetery.

A multitude awaited her.

Sebastian saw the risk in what he was showing her, but was there any choice? At least the dead who had never had a dream would show her what she might have been.

The dead Felicia saw were gray and still. They hovered by their graves as if chained to them, and the faces they turned to her were mournful. She walked among them like a queen, but she was queen of a cold kingdom.

"Why are they like that, Sebastian? Why do they stay? Why don't they speak?"

"They have no vision," Sebastian said.

"No vision?"

"In life they never dreamed of what they might become. They saw only the earth and the things that were upon it, and now that they are dead they are trapped here by their own blindness. They have never seen the path that they might take to set them free."

"Is there no help for them, Sebastian?"

"A few can be guided to find their way, and that has been my work here for as long as some men live."

"But if you can send them onward, then why are you still here, Sebastian?"

"Because of the choice I made almost four centuries ago. Because of the dark visions in my mind that make me fear I would find nothing but terror and torture on the far side of the grave."

Felicia held him closer. "Surely it would not be possible," she said, "for fate to be so cruel?"

"Fate is indifferent," Sebastian said, "and only humankind is cruel. We damn ourselves if we feel the need for our damnation. You could wander through these baffled souls all night and never find the man who died in my house an hour ago, for he was set in his hard ways, and most certainly dwells now in a hell of his own devising."

"And is there no way out, Sebastian?"

"None that I know of, for him or for me.

And none, I fear, for you, now that you have become my prisoner."

Sebastian pulled away from her, but Felicia took his arm again. The lights in the sky streamed down.

"What are you saying?" she asked him.

"No more than you already know. A spirit of sweet melancholy such as yours would certainly have found a kind of peace in death, while now you are condemned to wander the earth eternally in search of human blood. I know that you can feel the thirst already, and in time it will be more than you can bear."

Felicia stared at the army of the unhappy dead. "If not for you," she said, "I might have been one of these."

"If not for me," Sebastian replied, "you might have been free."

Felicia saw the small gray shadow of what must have been a child, and she turned toward it. "How could he be so young and have so little spirit in him?"

"A school, a church, a family. There are many ways. Something frightened him when he was alive, and now you will frighten him again."

Felicia ignored this warning and reached out to the boy as if to comfort him, but he ducked back from her touch and disappeared into the darkness of the cemetery.

"The dead will fear you as much as the living," Sebastian told her, "for we are alien to both."

"And yet you speak to them. . . ."

"Some may be drawn by spells, and rituals, and by a mingling of my will with their own, but this is no easy task. Making a true friend among the living is a simple thing compared to gaining the trust of a lost soul."

"I shall help with them as well, Sebastian. Think how many souls we shall set free."

"A pretty thought. But consider how many we shall slay, some of them irretrievably condemned to agony, in the time that it will take to turn even one of these blind creatures toward the light. The equation will not balance; the scales are tipped against us. I had a brother centuries ago, who thought himself a holy man. He took it as his task to seek out heretics, to torture and kill them so that their souls might be saved. He caused immeasurable suffering, but he thought he was justified. I did not believe it, and I do not believe it of myself. The undead see with much more clarity than that. I can argue that I seek to slay only those whose death might make the world a better place, but where is the transgressor half as great as I? It is the thirst that rules me, and it will rule you."

"No," Felicia said, "I will not drink."

229

"You are still innocent," Sebastian replied. "You will come to realize in time that the choice has been made for you. I have never known one of our kind who could resist the call of the blood for long."

"Then are there others?"

"I imagine there must be somewhere, but none that I could name. The others I have known were those that I created, and none of them survived."

Felicia gasped, and studied him with new terror in her glowing eyes. "You mean that they were like that boy? That you destroyed them all?"

"I do what I must," Sebastian said. "Many were lost through their own recklessness, and some of those I loved. It is a dreadful thing to be as we are, and full of peril. There is no creature on the earth more feared or more despised."

Felicia shuddered and embraced herself, but there was no warmth in her white arms. Her gown might have been gossamer, but the chill she felt did not come from the night. It was deep within her.

"I will not be a creature such as that," she finally said.

"You should have chosen when you could," Sebastian said. "But there is glory in it, too, Felicia. Only a few moments ago you saw some of the magic, and soon you will see more. Even what you fear the most has a kind of poetry in it. You are weak now, but soon you will feel a surge of power such as you have never known. The desire will lead you to it, and it will put an end to weakness and to doubt as well. Come, Felicia, let me show you!"

He pulled her away from the sea of gray faces that hovered around them, away from All Souls, and out into the London that was full of life. She resisted for a moment, but no longer, for inwardly she was eager to go: not, she told herself, because she longed for blood, but because she thirsted for something of the existence she had left behind, for the life that was still half hers. For the first time that she could recall, she wished to be away from death.

They walked through the sleeping streets of London. The hour was late, and not a person was in sight. The houses of the residential neighborhood were dark, and yet Felicia sensed each individual life within them; she could feel each heart beating, hear each quivering breath. Each building seemed to pulsate, and yet the thoroughfares were as empty as Felicia felt, part of a black wasteland. Without Sebastian's presence she would have gone mad.

They passed an old church, and Felicia wondered if it should have frightened her. It did not, strangely enough, until she saw the churchyard. What she saw there was like a vision of the pit.

Here the dead, trapped in this little plot of earth, were massed in piles and rows beyond all reckoning, crawling over and over one another like a nest of phosphorescent serpents. None slipped beyond the borders of the graveyard fence, and so the glowing horror bulked upward along the wall of the church until it seemed that it would reach the sky.

"Sebastian!" Felicia whispered. "What does this mean?"

"Economy," he said. "This is a practical city, and these small churchyards have existed for centuries. They would have been filled long ago, and indeed they were, leaving no room for the next generation's dead. So they were buried atop each other, year after year, century after century, the old bones crushed or cast aside, until each plot of land was like a city of the dead. If there had not been believers among this throng, the tower of torment that you see would reach up to the heavens. At least you have been spared this, Felicia. The acres of new cemeteries like All Souls prohibit such abominations as you see, at least for now, although of course, the men of London think to do no more than to eliminate the spread of pestilence. I wonder if the diseases they have learned to fear came from the bodies or the souls of these forgotten dead?"

Felicia hurried past the consecrated ground so quickly that Sebastian was left behind her for a moment. And as she rushed by a dark alley, Felicia was frozen into place by the unexpected sound of a shrill and grating laugh.

"Don't run so fast, love," screamed the voice from the darkness. "You'll have much more fun when he catches you!"

Felicia peered into the alley and saw a living woman; the sight was as great a shock as she had experienced in all that night. Such persons as the one before Felicia were not entirely unfamiliar to her, but she had always turned her eyes from them at once. Now she found herself fascinated.

The prostitute lay half sprawled on the damp earth, her back propped up against a dripping wall of stone. Her skirts had been pulled up almost to her waist, and a bottle was clutched in her right hand. Her face was so covered in powder and rouge that it might have been anyone's; nonetheless, it smiled at Felicia.

"Can't quite get up," the woman said apologetically. Felicia moved toward her, thinking only to offer aid. The woman reached out an arm to her. It was plump and ruddy. It seemed to glow with a rosy light. Felicia grasped it and suddenly realized that she would not be able to let go. This drunken, debauched woman had become the most desirable thing in all of creation. Her body throbbed with blood, and Felicia felt it course through each separate vein and artery. She pulled the harlot to her feet, and all at once the two of them were locked in an intoxicated but heartfelt embrace. Felicia felt her fingers running through the woman's hair and was overwhelmed by the welcome heat of her soft body. The woman kissed her clumsily.

"What about your old man, then?" she whispered.

The words themselves had less effect on Felicia than the sudden reek of the woman's breath, which was foul with more than the scent of gin. Her revulsion battled with her lust.

She twisted her head around and glimpsed Sebastian silhouetted against a gaslight at the end of the alley. His tall figure was motionless. He waited.

Felicia's head swam. Her teeth felt sharp, and her tongue dry. The thirst consumed her. Her hands went to the woman's throat, which was full almost to bursting. The merest touch would let loose a flood of bliss, a fountain of blood.

"The three of us could all have fun, you know, dear. Wouldn't your friend like that?"

Felicia's opened mouth snapped shut; her body stiffened. Slowly, painfully, she pushed the woman back against the wall.

"Did I say something wrong, dear?" the woman wailed. Felicia backed away. "Have you got any money?"

Felicia staggered down the alley into Sebastian's cold arms.

"Take her," he whispered. "What will she lose?"

The woman slumped against the wall and slithered toward the ground.

"What harm will it do?" Sebastian demanded. "She will be dead by morning in any case."

"No harm to her, perhaps," Felicia said, "but much harm to me."

"You must do it, my love, for your own sake."

"You have shown me such wonders, Sebastian, and now you would have me kill a woman."

"Would you rather kill a man?"

"Would that be any better?"

"Would it be any worse?"

"I will not do it!" Felicia shouted, her voice

so loud that it made the drunken woman stir in her sleep. Sebastian drew her away.

"Sooner or later you must drink," he said. "There is hardly a drop of blood left in you, and only that continues your existence."

"And if I do not drink?"

"You will drink."

"But if I do not?"

"Then your fate would be worse than any of those that we have seen this night. You would be incarcerated in a corpse too weak to move, condemned to a prison of frozen flesh for all eternity. You must not think of it."

"And if I do?"

"An endless agony of thirst. It must not come to that. The desire must prove stronger than your will."

He looked into the glow of her pale eyes and saw determination there, and yet there was a plea for mercy, too.

"And is there no way out?" Felicia asked him.

"A way out," Sebastian repeated. He peered into the sky. There was a fire in the east.

"Enough," Sebastian said mournfully. "Enough for now. Come away, Felicia. Come. It is the sun."

The Final Note

Nigel Stone paced through the empty rooms of the echoing house he shared with his cousin. He had been in the place for only a few days, but already its atmosphere oppressed him. He knew that Callender was upstairs somewhere, sleeping off what must have been an appalling headache, yet the mansion seemed utterly deserted, an abode fit for ghosts rather than for men. Out of sheer desperation Stone was tempted to drop off himself on the settee in the study that had served him as a bed, but he fought the temptation, though there was little enough for a man to do in London when he had no money and no friends. It wasn't even a fit day for a stroll around the old town, unfortunately; a heavy rain had been falling for most of the afternoon, interrupted from time to time by distant growls of thunder and dim glimmerings of lightning.

Still, Stone decided that a storm would be more stimulating than wandering through a house that seemed half haunted. He headed for the door, threw it open, and stared out into the street. The rain rattled down and splashed in the gutters; wind blew some of it into Stone's face. Across the way a man scrambled for shelter, and his antics made Stone feel very satisfied to be indoors after all. Yet something in the power of the elements made him feel strong and alive; he remembered how he had run shouting through storms when he had been a boy.

As he looked out on nature's fury, Stone saw a coach round a corner and pull up in front of the doorway that sheltered him. The horses steamed and shivered in the downpour. Stone felt a trifle foolish to be standing there but would have been even more ashamed to duck back inside like a frightened child, especially when the coachman jumped down from his perch, his high hat dripping, and scrambled up the steps to meet him. Stone did his best to act like a prosperous householder.

"Mr. Nigel Stone?" asked the coachman.

"What? Me?" stammered Stone. "Yes, of course it's me. What can I do for you, my good man?"

"A message for you from a lady, sir. She said to wait for an answer." He pulled a piece of paper from somewhere inside his soaking coat and handed it to Stone. The wet ink was already beginning to blur.

My Dear Mr. Stone,

Please come at once, and if you can, come without Mr. Callender. My niece Felicia has disappeared, and I fear for her safety. I believe I can rely on you, and no one else.

A drop of rain turned the signature to a gray smudge, but there could be no doubt about the name. Stone felt pleasure at the summons, and then a twinge of shame that he should take such delight in the misfortune of a young woman.

"I'll come at once," he said.

"Then come with me, sir. I'll wait here while you get your greatcoat."

"No need for that," mumbled Stone. He was embarrassed to confess that he owned no such garment but not quite desperate enough to pilfer his cousin's; he hoped the coachman would take his scanty costume as a sign of dedication rather than desperation. A blast of thunder ripped the sky apart as he hurried down the steps.

That same thunder woke Reginald Callender at last. He cursed, then sat up so quickly that he wrenched his back. His sheets were soaked with sweat, and they had begun to stink. He itched all over, and he started to tremble as soon as he awoke. When he heard the rain, he was seized with a wild desire to run naked into London and wash himself clean, but he had just enough judgment left to realize that this might not be wise.

Callender huddled under his quilts and pulled damp pillows over his head, trying without much success to shut out the world. Now that he was conscious again, he could not bear to lie awake alone with his own thoughts. Visions of doom hounded him even in his own bed. He could not stay there.

He crawled out into the clammy air and began to shiver. He called for the servants, even though he knew that they were gone. Then he called for his cousin Nigel, but there was no reply. He felt utterly abandoned.

The house was too big for him. He had a sudden, unreasoning fear of being a small speck in a vast space. It was unbearable.

He pulled on such clothes as he could find and took a pull from the bottle beside the bed.

He thanked heaven for his uncle's cellar, which was still his even if the house would soon be sold for debts, and he dreaded the day when the wine would run dry. He drank again and heard the rain battering against his window.

He hardly noted the weather, though, for his mind was in an uproar. There was a great need in him to escape from these walls and from his memories. Compared to them, a thunderstorm was a small thing.

A song rang through his head, a tantalizing tune that meant nothing yet said much. Against it, as a counterpoint, rang heavy sounds of resentment and recrimination, memories of an evening when he had said and done much that might not be forgiven. Much wiser, he thought, to follow the notes of the sweeter, shallower song, and to forget the rest. He felt in his pockets, found a few shillings, then staggered down the staircase and out the door to stand under the streaming skies. He had no cash for a cab, but he knew the way to The Glass Slipper on foot.

His journey was a vision. Water fell in curtains before him and rose in glistening fountains at every curb. Rainbows formed in every gaslight, and phantoms in the fog. His way was weary, but he was too tired to rest. From time to time the whirling wheels that

passed him covered him in water, but it was
no more to him than paint on lips that were
already scarlet. Drenched and deranged,
Reginald Callender made his way through
forgotten streets until he reached his remembered goal.

The glass globes over the flickering flames
at the entrance to The Glass Slipper seemed to
Callender like stars in the heavens. He stepped
over cigars, mud, and orange peels to reach
the arch where a shilling bought his way into
the saloon bar.

"Buy us a bottle of fizz?" Callender pushed
the drab out of his way and proceeded up into
the balcony. This had always been a disorderly
house, but now it struck him as the true home
of chaos. Each face he saw was a twisted
demonic shape, each voice a mockery of
human tone. He was vaguely aware that some
spurned him for the unshaven, sodden wretch
he had become, but it mattered little when he
knew he was so close to Sally Wood.

"Give your orders, gentlemen, please!" The
harsh voice cut through the tobacco fumes,
the smell of stale beer and cheap perfume. In
another life Callender would have ignored the
summons, but now that he was destitute he
felt compelled to buy a glass of beer. A girl
with plump arms and a vacant face offered to
sell him sweets from a glass jar but backed

away when she saw his expression. The orchestra struck up a tinny tune, one Callender recognized. The gods were with him after all. It was Sally's song.

Some girls place a price upon their maidenhood,
Defend it, never spend it till the price is good.
They wouldn't give a gent a tumble if they could.
They couldn't if they would,
They wouldn't if they could,
But everybody knows Sally Wood.

And there she was, in a gaudy red dress, strutting saucily across the stage. She bawled out her litany, her skirts hiked up to her garters, and Callender dreamed of what lay beyond them. He wondered how many men shared the same dreams, perhaps even the same memories, and he hated them all.

Someone clapped him on the back and handed him a glass of brandy; he didn't notice who it was. When Sally hit her final note and made a low curtsy in her low-cut dress, he stood stock-still and stared while every other man in The Glass Slipper gave vent to boisterous shouts and applause. He did not move as Sally leapt from the stage, wove her way expertly through the orchestra, pushed through the crowd with a few playful slaps, and hurried up to the balcony bar. She passed within a few feet of Callender on her way to the spot where a man with a swarthy face and black sidewhiskers was standing. There was a bottle of champagne beside him on the bar, and he poured Sally a glass as she approached, her face flushed and her chestnut hair flowing.

Callender awoke from his paralysis and stumbled toward Sally. She turned when he grasped her arm.

"Reggie!" she said, and then she laughed. "You do look a sight!"

"It's the rain."

"You'd better go home, dear, or you'll catch your death. I'll talk to you another night."

She turned her back on him.

"Sally! You'll talk to me now!" He reached out for her again, but the stranger put himself between them.

"You can see that the lady is occupied," he said. His tone was the one that Callender had been accustomed to use when talking to servants. Callender tried to push him away, but the man was like an oak.

Callender took a swing at the man, who ducked back without hesitation and then put a bony fist in his opponent's face.

Callender was surprised to find himself sitting on the floor. His nose and mouth felt hot and wet. There was laughter all around him.

He was trying to decide what to do when he had another shock: He saw Sally slap her escort's face. This brought another roar from the crowd, which burst into wilder applause than it had ever granted one of her songs when Sally knelt beside the stricken Callender and took him in her arms.

"Come on, Reggie," she said. "You're all right."

"Sally?"

"That's right, dear. You come along with me. Can't have my husband murdered, can I?"

Her words hardly registered as she helped him to his feet and out of the The Glass Slipper.

The rain was still falling, and Callender lifted his face toward it to wash away the blood. He hardly looked where he was walking, but he was conscious enough to remember that her lodgings were just around the corner from the music hall. He dragged his boots through a puddle like a child and found a kind of pleasure in it. He had begun to love the storm. When the thunder rumbled, he made the same sort of noise himself. Sally looked at him and smiled.

She led him up two flights of stairs and into her disordered room, as full of jumble as his own dwelling was barren, then sat him down on her unmade bed. It was covered with clothes. He saw a pamphlet, half hidden by a dress, and picked it up.

"Still reading penny dreadfuls, Sal?"

"Oh, you mean the vampire. You should take that along, Reggie. I'm finished with that bit, and it's awfully good."

Callender shrugged and stuffed the thing into his pocket. His mind was fuddled, but somewhere in it was the glimmer of an idea. There was something else, too, something he wanted to remember.

"Look here. What was that you said to me back at the Slipper, eh?"

"What do you mean, dear? Take off your coat. It's wet."

"Leave me alone. I want to be wet."

"Have it your own way, then," said Sally, peeling off her gown and posing before him in her corset. "I just wanted to get you warm."

"Warm, is it? And what did you say back there about a husband?"

She sat beside him and ran her tongue across his lips. "Only that a girl has to take care of her intended, Reggie."

He looked at her blearily. "You must be mad," he said.

"Not half, I'm not. You promised to marry me, right here in this very bed, you did, and I mean to hold you to it, Mr. Reggie Callender."

"Dreaming," he said.

"What?"

"One of us is dreaming. Whatever made you think that I would marry you?"

"You did, dear. When your uncle died, you said, and you were wealthy in your own right, you'd make an honest woman of me. And now he's dead, ain't he? I can see you took it hard, with your kind heart, but that will pass, and then we'll be wed. You do love me, don't you, dear? There's nobody else?"

He fumbled at her, more out of habit than passion. "Of course there's nobody else," he said.

"No?" Sally pushed him down on the bed and slapped him harder than she had the man in The Glass Slipper. "And what about Miss Felicia Lamb?"

Callender was too stunned to reply.

"You think I'm stupid, don't you? You thought I didn't know about her! What do you take me for?"

Callender just sat on the bed and looked across the room.

"Here," said Sally. "Have some gin." She pulled a bottle from a pile of dresses in a corner and gave it to Callender. He uncorked

247

it and poured half of it down his throat.

"That's right," said Sally. "Get yourself used to the idea. You thought I was just a silly girl. That's what you think of all of us, ain't it? And that's why we do what we can to protect ourselves. You recollect a girl named Alice? Your uncle's maid. We were good friends, Alice and me. She told me all about you. Now, I don't begrudge you your bit of fun, Reggie. I've had mine. We'll forget Alice, even if she has seen more of your uncle's money than ever I did. But I won't let you marry this Felicia Lamb."

Callender took another pull on the bottle and put his head in his hands. The liquor burned against his bleeding gums. This was hardly the evening he had planned.

"I saw her once, you know," Sally said. "A blueblood virgin with big eyes and a tiny mouth. She's no woman for a man like you. I'll bet she wouldn't even raise her skirt to piss!"

It was Callender's turn to slap Sally. Then he picked up his hat and his stick and shuffled toward the door. "She is the woman I love," he said.

"Love, is it?" shouted Sally. "See how much love you find there after today, Mr. Callender! She'll have nothing to do with you now! You're mine! Do you think I spent two years on my back for the pure pleasure of it?" She rushed to follow him, shouting in his ear.

Callender summoned up a drunken dignity. "There is nothing you can do to prevent this marriage," he said. "You and I shall not meet again."

"I've stopped you already," Sally screamed. "I sent her a note, that's what I did. A letter telling her what you have been to me. She'll have read it by now, and that'll be an end to any love between you!"

Callender staggered back against the door. To have lost two fortunes in so short a time was more than he could bear. Without thinking, without even wishing to, he slammed his ebony walking stick into Sally's face.

She seemed bewildered, and she made a whimpering sound. He saw by the candlelight that he had turned her right eye into red pulp.

She put her hand to her face, and something came away in it. She dropped to her knees and began to wail.

Callender was horrified. He stooped to help her, but she pushed him away and crawled across the floor. She began to scream.

It was intolerable. He hit her again, this time on the top of her head, but it only made her scream louder.

He struck her twice more. The stick broke, and Sally slumped to the floor. The screaming stopped.

Callender ran down the stairs and into the street. In an alley, in the rain, he vomited again and again. At first he thought it would kill him, but when he was done his head began to clear. The storm was lifting, and the gleams of lightning seemed to come from miles away.

He was almost home when he realized that he was holding only half of his walking stick. He gazed at the jagged stump in disbelief. He tried to convince himself that he had dropped the other half somewhere in the street, but he felt a sick certainty that it was lying beside Sally Lamb. Could it be used to identify him? Callender had heard of the detective inspectors newly appointed to Scotland Yard, and of the tricks they could play in catching criminals of every kind. He could not take the chance of leaving anything behind.

The journey back was agonizing. He wanted nothing less than to visit Sally Lamb again, yet speed seemed imperative since he knew her corpse would be discovered eventually. He had to be there and gone again before it was. He could not bear to think of what would happen if he were caught with her body, yet he could not think of anything else. He wanted a drink. He was half tempted to hurry home for one, yet all the while his feet were carrying him back to The Glass Slipper. His thoughts were so agitated that he found himself there before he was quite prepared.

Several loungers stood outside, and the faint sound of music came from within. It was as if nothing had happened. Could it be that they did not yet know?

The thought froze Callender for an instant, then he backed into the shadows of an alley. For the first time in his life he was afraid to be seen. Yet it was madness to remain here, a few feet from his crime but doing nothing to conceal it. He pulled down his hat and turned up his collar as if seeking protection from the rain, then stepped casually into the street and walked briskly around the corner.

He looked up at Sally's solitary window, where a light still burned. There was no hue and cry, no sign of anything amiss. He pushed the street door open cautiously, thanking whatever power protected him that he had neglected to close anything behind him in his hurry to be gone. He crept up the stairs, his ear cocked for the slightest sound. The house was as still, he thought wryly, as a tomb.

And so it remained until he reached Sally's

door. The sound he heard behind it gave him a chill the rain could not. He knew it must be his imagination, some symptom of a guilty conscience, but he would have sworn he recognized the melody of the song Sally had performed at The Glass Slipper not more than an hour before. Someone seemed to be humming it.

Could this be a ghost? Another trick of that damned spiritualist? He didn't believe it. He couldn't. It had to be a trick of his own mind. A small thing, really, and he needed the rest of that stick.

He opened the door.

What he saw was worse than what he feared. Sally, her face awash with blood and her pretty hair matted down with it, was crawling on her hands and knees around the room, singing her song as best she could through lips that dribbled blood. She had not died after all, but she might have been better off if she had.

Sally knocked over a table, and still she sang her song. Callender realized that he had damaged her beyond repair. She had no idea that he was in the room.

His mouth twitched uncontrollably as he raised his boot and brought it down with all his weight on the back of Sally's neck. He heard her spine snap.

He needed the last of the gin he stole from her room.

He picked up the other half of his walking stick and hurried home to bed, where he spent the next three days attempting to convince himself that he had never left it.

FIFTEEN

The Heiress

Three men dressed in blue gathered in front of a tall brick house near the gates of All Souls Cemetery. Their high hats held sturdy metal frames, and their knee-length coats had buttons made of brass. In each man's belt was a wooden staff; one of them used his to knock on the door.

They waited in the darkness and the damp. One of them shivered in the cold. "There's no one here." he said. "We should have come by day."

"And so we have, some of us, but we had no answer then, anymore than we have now."

"We could break down the door."

"We're only seeking information from a gentleman. The people have little enough use for Scotland Yard without us making a name for ourselves as housebreakers."

"Then knock again."

"I'll give the orders here," said the man with the staff, but he used it again anyway.

A light appeared in one of the windows.

"We've roused someone."

"Be still, will you?"

The door opened slowly and silently; a tall man with a black mustache appeared on the threshold, a black candle in his hand. Its flickering light gleamed unpleasantly on the long scar that ran down the left side of his face.

"Good evening sir. I hope we have not disturbed you."

"I have been sleeping, constable. What brings you here?"

"A woman, sir. Miss Felicia Lamb."

"I do not see her with you."

"No, sir. She's not to be seen anywhere, and that's what concerns us. Are you Mr. Newcastle, sir?"

"I am."

"Well, sir, we've been informed that Miss Lamb was a frequent visitor here, and since she's vanished, we've taken it upon ourselves to make inquiries. We'd be most appreciative of any help."

"I see. Tell me, constable, how long has she been missing?"

"Just four days. It's Monday, and she was last seen on Thursday night, at a dinner party."

"It has been longer than that since I have seen Miss Lamb, constable. Have you spoken to the people who dined with her?"

"Two of them, sir. Her aunt, who mentioned you to us, and a friend of the family, a Mr. Nigel Stone. The third member of the party was her betrothed, a Mr. Callender. We have visited him several times but found nobody home."

"Perhaps they have run away together."

"Yes. We thought of that. But why should they elope when they were already pledged?"

"From what I have seen of Mr. Callender, he is a most headstrong young man."

"So we have been told. You know him, sir?"

"We have met twice. And even on such short acquaintance I could not form a high opinion of his character."

"As you say, sir. We've had reports that he'd been drinking heavily."

"Just so. Is there more that I can do for you, constable? Would you care to search for Miss Lamb within?"

Sebastian Newcastle stepped aside and gestured into the black recesses of his home.

The three men from Scotland Yard looked into the darkness and then at one another.

"Well, sir," said their leader. "Since you've been good enough to offer, it follows that we needn't bother you tonight. Clearly you have nothing to hide."

"Then may I bid you good night, gentlemen? The hour is late."

"Just so, sir. Thanks for your trouble, and good night to you."

Sebastian shut the door and stood for a few moments with nothing to keep him company but the small flame of his candle. When he knew that the men had gone, he turned into the dark depths of the house and called for Felicia, but knew before he spoke that there would be no answer. She could not be constrained at night; she wandered, ever weaker, through the valley of stones where the dead slept.

Sebastian went out into the night. He dissolved into an iridescent fog before the cemetery gates and drifted into All Souls, part of the thick mist that made the land look like a forgotten sea whose turbulence hid all but the wreckage of tortured trees and abandoned monuments. The landscape was more like a limbo for unhappy spirits than a part of the green earth.

He found Felicia sitting on a monument, her pale arms wrapped around the marble figure of an angel, her pale eyes staring off into the fog.

"Three men came to look for you," he said.

"And did three men leave?"

"Since they came from Scotland Yard, it seemed unwise to detain any of them."

"Police," Felicia said. "Have I destroyed your sanctuary here, Sebastian?"

"Perhaps, but that matters little when I see you as you are."

"I am as I wished to be."

"And was it worth it, then, to see life and death as two sides of the same coin, and to hold that coin in your own hand?"

"I have learned much," Felicia said.

"You have learned more than you bargained for. The price of that coin is blood."

Felicia hugged herself and looked down at the ground. "I cannot, Sebastian," she said.

"And yet you must," he said, "and most assuredly you will. The lives of others must become your life, and their blood your own. It is your fate, and none may resist it."

"I shall. I swear it. You know what I am now, better than any other could, but whatever I have become, I am still innocent of blood. I shall not stain my soul with it."

Sebastian turned away from her. She rose

and took his arm. "I meant no reproach to you," she said.

"Then I must reproach myself. As you have said, I know what will become of you. You will grow weaker, and the thirst will grow stronger, until at length you will be transformed into the thirst. You saw how long I could resist you, for all my wish to do so."

"You did what I desired you to do," Felicia said.

"I would have done it anyway!"

Sebastian took her beautiful pale face into his cold hands. "You came to me as my bride," he said, "and I have been alone too long. Now I must see to it that you survive."

"Is there no other way?"

"If you can resist the thirst, then it will doom you. Your body will become too frail to move, but still it will contain your soul. Your spirit will never be free to seek the worlds beyond our own. It will be trapped in a lifeless husk, and you will be truly damned."

She gazed deeply into his dark eyes, then stiffened in his arms at the sound of a human voice nearby.

A lantern gleamed dully through the yellow fog.

"Three men," she said long before she could see them.

"The constables," Sebastian said.

"Then let us greet them and be done with this." She laughed loudly and bitterly.

Three dark figures emerged from the mist, clustering around their light as if they feared to lose it.

"Mr. Newcastle," one of them said.

Sebastian bowed slightly but made no reply.

"And Miss Felicia Lamb?"

"What is that to you?" Felicia snapped.

"Your aunt said you were lost, miss."

"And now I am found."

"Just so, miss. But look where we've found you. In a graveyard, at night, and with nothing to cover you but a nightgown."

"This is my mother's wedding dress."

"Oh, I see. A wedding dress, is it? A runaway heiress and a foreign gentleman. You weren't quite honest with us, were you, Mr. Newcastle?"

"Sometimes a gentleman must keep his tongue, constable," Felicia said. "Though you seem to know nothing of that."

"No, miss, I'm no gentleman, right enough. Just a rough fellow trying to do his job. Still, I offer our protection if you ask for it. This is no fit place for a young lady, and no fit company if I'm any judge."

"You may never live to be a judge," Sebastian said. He cast his eye on the lantern in the constable's hand. At once its faint flame turned a blazing red; the metal became too hot to hold. The man screamed in anguish as he dropped the light; suddenly there was only blackness and the smell of burning flesh.

"There is danger in the dark," Sebastian said as he moved forward. He felt Felicia's grip on his shoulder and saw her pale eyes imploring him to stop. Together they watched the three men scramble away through the tombstones and the trees. At last there was silence.

"There will be danger from them," Sebastian finally said. "We might have feasted, and now we must flee. Was it wise for you to stop me?"

"I stopped you because I wanted nothing more than to let you go. To join you, in fact. The one on the right, the young one. I wanted him."

"He was yours, Felicia. He can be yours in a moment."

"No, Sebastian. It must not be. I cannot do what you have done. I never thought of it. I dreamed only of death, and peace, and freedom. I wanted knowledge, not the power to destroy."

"There is more to know," Sebastian said, "and time enough to know it, but only if you take life."

She pulled back from him and leaned

against a marble slab engraved with the name of one long dead. She had never seemed more beautiful to him, and never more beloved, than when she renounced all that he could offer her.

"You have thrown away the mortal life that you were born to live," he said. "If you throw away this second chance, there will be nothing left for you but an eternity of emptiness."

"Would that be so different from what you endure?"

"At least I still exist. I walk the earth. What could be more precious?"

"Then this is all your magic offers you? The chance to walk the earth like other men?"

"Other men die," Sebastian said.

Felicia reached out to him, took one step forward, and then sank to her knees. "Help me," she murmured.

He looked down at her compassionately. "You must not kneel to me," he said, "or any man."

"I did not do it willingly," she said. "I cannot stand."

"You must have blood, and you must have it now."

"No," she said. "Too late. No blood. No life."

She sank into the damp grass. Sebastian hovered over her; he tried to raise her to her feet. He kissed her; he shouted at her.

Nothing mattered. She could not be awakened.

Sebastian swept her up in his arms and moved toward his house, but he realized at once that the men would be waiting for him there. He turned back toward the stones, toward the tombs he had guarded for many years, but there was no consolation in them. He searched her face for some faint flicker of life and saw nothing but cold perfection. Yet he knew that her soul was trapped within her corpse and would remain there until time stopped.

He put her to rest in a tomb and raged through the night. Dogs howled, marble shattered like glass, and three men who trembled in the night fog came to the decision that their investigations might be best conducted in the light of day.

S I X T E E N

Voyagers

Callender found himself down by the docks again.

He had not meant to venture there, certainly not at night, and what was worse, he could not remember why he had come. The fog was so thick that he might have been anywhere for all that he could see, but he recognized the sounds of the river: water lapping against the pilings of decaying wood, the faint creak of distant rigging, and the mournful cry of a foghorn. He could even hear music from a tavern, so faint that he could not make out the tune, and the reek of the Thames at low tide was unmistakable.

The scent seemed to mingle with the sounds somehow, as if they were one, and

Callender felt that he could taste the fog. All his senses were confused and intermingled. He smelled darkness, and each sound seemed to touch him like a blow. Every stimulus around him was unnaturally intensified, and yet he was as good as blind.

Lost, frightened, and bewildered, Callender stumbled toward the river. He tried to remember what had brought him there. He could not even recall when he had taken his last drink, and though he doubted that he was sober, he felt less like a drunkard than a man in a dream.

He hoped he would awaken soon.

He glimpsed a flash of whiteness in the mist and saw the shadow of a human figure. It might have been a woman.

"Wait," Callender whispered. "Please. I don't know where I am."

He was shocked to realize how little volume his voice had; he could hardly hear himself. Yet the figure in the fog seemed to pause for just a moment, as if perhaps Callender's call had touched it as the distant music in the night had touched him. Whoever it was turned toward him and then scurried away.

Callender ran after the woman. His steps dragged as if his feet were mired in the fog, and his greatest effort seemed to bring him no closer to his goal, but Callender pressed on, for the brief glimpse he had seen of the figure's pale face and golden hair had been enough to tantalize him. He thought he knew who it might be.

"Felicia," he gasped, the word choking in his throat.

Again she responded, and this time when she cast a glance at him, he recognized her with a shock that was echoed in her own expression.

Then she was gone.

Callender cried out again, but now he could produce no sound at all. The effort that it took to speak came close to strangling him. The fog was in his lungs, clogging them as surely as it tangled his feet. The air turned thicker, but he struggled forward with a desperation he did not entirely understand.

There was something in his mind about a letter that must be retrieved, and more about a fortune that must be saved, but stronger than either of these was a longing for Felicia herself, for the sound of her low voice, the touch of her cool hand. He had never thought, until she was lost to him, that he might love her.

His desire pushed him forward, and his longing for Felicia seemed to clear away the mist that billowed from the murky surface of the Thames. He heard his steps booming hollowly on the wooden planks of a decrepit dock, and all at once the fog around him cleared.

A ship waited on the river.

She was an elegant, trim craft, not large but somehow out of place in the murky waters near Limehouse. Her white sails glowed in the moonlight that suddenly broke through the clouds, her planks gleamed with a rich polish, and her fittings glistened with cold silver. The ship was an icy flame, and its reflection was a topsy-turvy shimmering on the black river.

The ship was Felicia, Callender thought, and yet Felicia was aboard.

He had no idea how she had reached the deck. The ship was well out in the water, much too far away for Felicia to have boarded in the few seconds since he had last seen her.

He stretched out his arms to her and tried to speak. She was alone, drifting, and she might be in danger, or so Callender thought at first. Then he noticed other figures on the deck.

Felicia stood by the bow. She might have been a figurehead, except that she continually looked back. Callender tried to convince himself that she had her eyes on him despite the shadowy figure of the helmsman hunched over the ship's gigantic wheel. It was to this sinister sailor that Felicia seemed to be directing her attention, and Callender might have followed her example if he had not noticed a group of others gathered amidships. He imagined that they had come up from below. What other explanation could there be?

The ship streamed away down the dark river, and Callender rushed to the end of the pier to follow its progress. The people on the deck were as small as puppets, yet he recognized them so certainly that he could not doubt the testimony of his eyes.

The first was his uncle William.

The old man danced and capered across the deck to the ship's rail. Callender knew that there was something wrong in all of this, but what it was escaped him.

"Reginald, my boy!" Uncle William's voice sounded miles away, yet every syllable was crystal clear. "Come on, son! We're leaving you! You'll miss the boat!"

Callender staggered at the edge of the pier, only inches of wood between him and the water. Another of the passengers whirled to beckon him.

"Jump, Reggie!" she called. "Jump, for a bit of fun!" Even at the distance he recognized the sweet shape of Sally Wood, and noticed that one side of her face was black and red.

Tears forced their way into his eyes. He was beginning to remember.

"That's right," came a hoarse reminder from a shattered body that shambled to the ship's rail. They were all drifting away, but this was clearly Samuel Sayer, too wounded and twisted to be anything but dead.

"That's right!" Sayer shouted. "We're dead! All dead! Come on, boy! Catch a ride!"

The fog was closing in again, narrowing the universe down to a meager band of shimmering river, with Callender standing at one end and a disappearing ship at the other. Something was becoming clear to him, too late for him to act. If this was a ship of the dead, then why was Felicia on it?

He had to save her life. He took one step forward and dropped into deep water.

Callender sank into silence. The bottom of the Thames was like a dream, a refuge from the horrors that lurked above. For a time he swam, becoming one with the depths, then he pulled himself toward the surface once again.

The ship seemed miles away. By now Callender believed that he was in a dream, and so set out for the craft as if any poor swimmer might catch it. If nothing else mattered, then one last effort might be worth a try.

Callender's arms flailed in futile pursuit of the phantom ship. He was consumed by a growing conviction that this was no more than a nightmare, but he was determined to see it through to the end. He dropped into the darkness more than once, and each time it tempted him. What was he struggling for? Felicia? Himself?

He broke the clean surface of the deadly water once again, and far behind him came the faint echo of voices shouting. Callender twisted his head while he struggled forward, and he saw two tiny figures on the distant dock that he had left behind. As small as insects, but just as insistent, the vision of two human beings forced itself upon him: his cousin Nigel, and Felicia's aunt Penelope. They were arm in arm, and they were radiant with a happiness that Callender had never even imagined.

He cursed them for it.

"Good-bye, old fellow!" shouted Nigel Stone. "And good luck to you!"

Callender forced his way against the tide. For a moment he thought he might be gaining, and then the shimmering ship ripped free of the river and soared into the stars.

Callender's fingers clawed at the empty air. The ship was lost to him, and he was too far from the shore. The river would be his final home. As he sank into it, however, he was allowed one last vision of the dark helmsman whose huge hands twisted the wheel of the spirit ship.

What he saw was not a revelation, only a confirmation. Sebastian Newcastle was the pilot of the vessel that had left him to drown.

Callender dropped into darkness, an insistent pounding ringing in his ears.

S E V E N T E E N

The Wine Cellar

Reginald Callender awoke to the sound of a distant and insistent banging. It came from far enough away so that it drifted slowly into his consciousness, becoming part of his dreams before it ended them. He was striking something again and again with his cane.

Then he was staring at his ceiling. His head throbbed with each repeated blow on the door downstairs, but Callender only cursed quietly and waited for the noise to stop. He wondered what day it was, and even if it were day at all. He raised one crusted eyelid and saw a stray shaft of sunlight break through the drawn curtains. Then he went back to sleep.

The next time he was disturbed, there was no putting it off. Someone had him by the shoulders and was shaking him more savagely than the aftermath of drink could ever do. A splash of cold water hit him in the face. Callender shouted, sputtered, and looked up into the ruddy face of his cousin.

"God damn you, sir," Callender roared. "Have you gone completely mad?"

"You call me mad, do you? It's Tuesday morning. Where have you been for five days, eh? Do you know what's happened to the girl you're going to marry?"

"What? Sally?"

"Who's Sally? What are you talking about? I mean Miss Lamb!"

"Felicia. Of course. I went to see her . . . when was it? But the servants said that she was not at home to me."

"She wasn't at home to anyone, my dear fellow. She has been missing for the best part of a week."

Callender pulled himself to a sitting postion. "How long has she been gone?"

"Since last Thursday. The night we had dinner at her house. The night I came to visit you."

"It's been a short enough visit, then, hasn't it? Where have you been ever since? And where's that bottle? My head!"

Callender felt under his bed and came up with what he sought.

"I thought you'd finished all the brandy," Stone said.

"So I did. But there's plenty of port. And now there's cause to celebrate as well. Felicia could never have read that letter, could she?"

"Letter? What letter?"

"A note from someone who wanted to drive us apart. Has anyone seen it?"

"Who cares for letters at a time like this?" demanded Stone.

"No, of course not." Callender took a drink of wine. "And you say Felicia's gone?

"Well, we did have some word of her."

"We?"

Stone's face turned a bit redder. "I've been with her aunt. Miss Penelope. She's terribly concerned, of course."

"Oh? You've been busy. The wealthy niece is missing, and all at once you're lodging in an elegant house with her spinster aunt."

"I'm doing what should have been done by you," Stone replied defensively. "Have you been locked in this empty house for all these days?"

"Of course I've been here," said Callender. "Where else would I have been?"

"That's what I decided, finally, even though those fellows from Scotland Yard were here more than once and said there wasn't a soul about."

Callender nearly dropped his bottle, and after he caught it he took a long drink. "Scotland Yard?"

"We naturally called them in when we couldn't find the girl, and they just as naturally sought to make inquiries of the man she's going to marry. I think they were a bit suspicious of you until they got some information."

"Thank God for that," said Callender. He sagged back on the bed. "Then I'm not suspected."

"Of course not! Look here, cousin, what's wrong with you? You don't seem to care what's happened to Felicia. Don't you want to hear what's become of her? She's been seen."

Stone paced indignantly across the room while Callender attempted to collect his thoughts. "Then she's safe?" he asked.

"I suppose you could say that, according to the law, but if you ask me, I'd say she was in mortal danger. She was seen with that man Newcastle."

Callender leapt from the bed, still half dressed in trousers and a soiled shirt. "Newcastle!" he shouted. He grasped his cousin by the collar and stared wildly into his eyes. "What has he done with her?"

"I don't know, I'm sure," said Stone as he disengaged himself. "But the constables said she was wearing what she called a wedding gown."

"Didn't they stop her? Didn't they take her away with them? My God!"

"Well. They said there was no law against a girl getting married if she had a mind, or taking a walk with her husband in the night air, if it came to that. Even if it was in a graveyard. And I think he did something to frighten them."

Callender snatched up a coat that had been thrown over a chair and began to rummage through its pockets. Half of a broken walking stick rattled to the floor, but he ignored it. At last he found a bedraggled little book and waved it at his cousin with an air of triumph. He sat down heavily in the chair and began turning pages with intense concentration. "He's done for me," he muttered. "And now I'll do for him."

"Look here, Reggie," began Stone.

"Be quiet, you fool! Can't you see I'm reading?"

"I can see I'm no use here," said Stone, more baffled than ever when he saw his cousin reach for the broken stick and clutch it triumphantly. "I'll let myself out. When you come to your senses, if you do, perhaps you'll do something to help us save Miss Lamb."

He strode from the room and was halfway down the stairs when he heard Callender raving at him, or perhaps at the world.

"Save her? I'll save her! I'm the only who can! I'm the only one who knows how!"

Nigel Stone never looked back. He locked the front door behind him and stepped out into the afternoon, the first he had seen with even a touch of sun since his arrival in London. He was content to take it as an omen. Elopements there might be, or even abductions, and madness certainly, but what did they matter? He was on his way to meet Miss Penelope Lamb, and for his own part he was happy.

A few minutes later Reginald Callender came out of the same door and squinted into the same sunlight. His hair was disheveled, his cravat awry, his gait unsteady. He tried to hail a cab, but the first two drivers merely glanced at him and passed by. A third pulled to a stop a few yards down the street, and Callender staggered after him. The cabman looked down from his perch.

"Let's see the color of your money before you climb aboard," he said.

Callender was obliged to go through his pockets once again. He pulled out Sally's penny dreadful, one half of the broken walking stick, and then the other. A small flask completed the catalog of his possessions.

"Looks like you'll be walking," said the cabman as he trotted off.

Callender hurled *Varney the Vampire* after the retreating cab. "I don't need this anymore," he screamed. "And I don't need you!"

He was suddenly aware that he had attracted the attention of several passersby and that he was standing in the middle of a tranquil street wailing like a fishwife. He recognized a neighbor who had been accustomed to tip his hat but now ostentatiously looked away. Callender saw the two sharp sticks and the flask that he had been waving in the air. He thrust them back into his coat and hurried away.

It was a long walk to All Souls Cemetery.

Callender's mind raced faster than his feet could carry him, but his thoughts ran in circles. He had lost everything: his fortune, his mistress, his bride, and her fortune, too. The list ran through his mind like a litany, and he began to suspect that he was losing his senses as well. In fact, he thought that he might welcome it if he could go completely mad, when his only alternative was to live in a world where he was besieged by devils.

At least he knew who was to blame. Newcastle had even produced his uncle's ghost, and by this time Callender was more than

willing to believe that somehow the spiritual-
ist had plundered his uncle's estate as well.
But Newcastle wasn't a spiritualist, of course.
He was a vampire.

The explanation seemed so simple to
Callender now. Hadn't he heard Felicia holding forth on vampires just before she disappeared? Still, the one he really had to thank
was Sally Wood, whose lurid little books on
the subject had revealed not only the cause of
his troubles but a remedy for them. And if not
a remedy, then at least revenge. Callender felt
a twinge of pity when he thought of Sally; he
wished he could have killed her quickly.

His next killing would have to be quick
whether he wished it or not. As he approached Newcastle's house, he saw that the
sun was low in the sky behind the trees of All
Souls. Could it really be that the dead would
rise soon?

He hurried toward Sebastian Newcastle's
house, but what he saw there disturbed him
even more than the setting sun. Before the
entrance stood a man dressed in a long blue
coat with brass buttons. Clearly the house was
under the surveillance of Scotland Yard.

Callender hesitated. His plan had been to
ransack the place, find Newcastle's undead
corpse, and bury his broken cane in it, but this

would hardly be possible under the circumstances. He might get some information from the constable on guard, but he hardly liked the idea of presenting himself to the law when he was a murderer himself. Should he risk it, or should he run?

His mouth was dry. He found the flask in his pocket and drained most of the port; the rest of it spilled down the front of his coat. The drink gave him courage enough to approach the house and find out what he needed to know. He made an effort to regain his dignity, walking very carefully as he approached the lair of his nemesis. He decided as he took the last few steps that aggression might be more effective than supplication.

"What's going on here?" he said. "Where's Mr. Newcastle?"

"That's what we'd like to know, sir. What's your business with him?"

"He's eloped with my fiancée. Is that business enough?"

"Are you Mr. Callender? We've been wanting to talk to you. What do you know about all this?"

"Nothing but what I've been told. I quarreled with Miss Lamb, about nothing really, and now I hear that this man has spirited her away. Have you any word of her?"

"No more than that, sir. She was seen with him once, in that graveyard yonder, but only then, and only for a moment."

"And have you searched the house?" demanded Callender.

"From top to bottom, sir."

"Are you certain? This is a strange house, you know," said Callender. "One night when I was here, the very walls seemed to dissolve into a fog."

"Indeed, sir! I've had nights like that myself. You seem to be having one now, if I may say so, and it ain't even night yet."

Callender ran the back of his hand over his dry lips. "How would you feel?" he asked. "What would you do? If I find this man Newcastle, I'll kill him."

"Well, sir, as to that, if a man ran off with my old woman, I'd buy him a drink! Eh? We mustn't take these things too serious." The constable paused, then squinted at Callender as if seeing him for the first time. "You wouldn't kill a lady, would you, sir?"

Callender swallowed hard. "Whatever do you mean?" he stammered. "Of course not!"

"Sometimes gentlemen lose their heads, in a manner of speaking. And Miss Lamb can't be found, you know."

"You're a fool," said Callender, turning on his heel.

"That's as may be, sir," the constable shouted at Callender's retreating back. "Will we find you at home, if something should turn up?"

Callender hurried off without bothering to reply. He could hardly have controlled himself for another second, especially when the talk of killing women started. The man seemed to be an ignorant commoner, but who could tell?

As he passed the cemetery once again, Callender noticed that the gates were open. He paused before them and peered in. This was where Felicia had been only a few hours before. If she and Newcastle were not in the house, might they not still be here? Callender entered All Souls.

The place was peaceful in the twilight, almost like a park with its green grass and gently rolling hills. Birds sang in the trees and perched on figures of white marble. This was a city of the dead, and Callender hardly knew which way to turn. Rows of effigies and headstones stretched in every direction; in the distance lay clusters of white mausoleums.

Almost helplessly, he moved along the streets of marble toward his uncle William's tomb. There his torment had started; perhaps it would end there, too. He had a vision, half inspired by Sally's cheap fiction, of rushing to that pale edifice and finding Felicia imprisoned there, the victim of a villain he could vanquish with one blow of his ebony stick. He longed to be a hero almost as much as he longed for another drink. He prayed to be free of his nightmare.

When he reached his goal, however, he found an avenging angel posed before it. Sitting in front of his uncle's final resting place was another man dressed in blue. His left hand was wrapped in bandages.

"Mr. Callender," he said. "Paying your last respects?"

"I don't know you," said Callender as he backed away.

"We should be better acquainted, then. What brings you here this evening?"

It took Callender some time to find his tongue. "I'm told Miss Lamb was seen here," he finally said.

"At this very spot? Who told you that? None of my men, I'll warrant you."

"This is the only spot I know," said Callender. "My uncle is interred behind you."

"I see. And does he lie alone?"

"Is there someone else?" gasped Callender. "Felicia? Newcastle?"

"Neither of those, sir," said the chief constable.

"Then where are they?"

"We don't know yet." The chief constable
stood up. "But we do know there are two
bodies in that tomb that don't belong there,
both of them horribly mutilated. The bodies
of two young boys. What do you make of that,
Mr. Callender, sir?"

Callender backed away, almost convinced
that this was another of his drunken dreams.
The man from Scotland Yard stared at him.
Callender wheeled around and ran.

Running suited him, Callender decided. His
lungs rasped, his heart thumped, and his
stomach churned, but he was leaving everything behind him. When he glanced back, the
immobile man in blue had dwindled to a tiny
figure, no more threatening than a toy soldier.

Still, under darkening skies, Callender ran.
He ran past monuments and mausoleums,
through iron gates, then down streets where
living men and women walked who scattered
at the sight of him. He tumbled into the gutter
once, and when he rose he was face-to-face
with a lamplighter on his rounds. "So soon?"
screamed Callender as he raced on.

He knew that he must be home before night
fell.

He could hardly believe his good fortune
when he reached the ugly, empty house that
was his sanctuary. He fumbled for his key and
howled in agony when it was nowhere to be

found. In panic he pounded on the door, then to his amazement felt it open for him. Dimly, he recalled that he had never had his key and never locked the house. He slammed the door on the sunset and turned the bolt behind him. He was safe.

Callender sank to his knees in the dark hallway. He was ruined, and he acknowledged it. He wandered through the hollow rooms while the last rays of the day died outside. He was on the verge of tears, and he hated himself for that. The tears might have been for Felicia Lamb, or for Sally Wood, or even for his uncle William, but all these had betrayed him. Callender wept for himself.

It made no difference.

He beat his hands against bare walls; he cursed the universe. It did not care.

At length his desolation brought him to himself, which was all that he had left to him. It was not enough. He could at least have a bottle to keep him company.

In the last week he had learned the way to the wine cellar. He thought he might take residence there, among the dusty bottles and the crates of cloth his cousin had brought back from India. He could make a bed for himself in the worthless textiles, and the wine would be close at hand. The idea pleased him. He made his way through the kitchen, then the pantry, where he found the stub of a candle to light his way.

The dark stairs were old friends to him, and the dark vault that he reached was refuge. He found the shelves where the old port rested and picked the best vintage left to him. He broke off the top of the bottle and poured the rich red liquid down his throat. He had to spit out a chip of glass, but it had only cut his lip.

He sat down in the dust and looked around. He drank again, at the same time noticing that something had been disturbed. One of the heavy boxes from India had been removed from the pile and set in the middle of the cellar. Its lid was loose.

Callender approached it cautiously. He left the candle on the floor, to keep both hands free. As soon as he touched the top of the box, it clattered to the stones below.

There seemed to be nothing more inside than bolts of dyed cotton, but Callender was dissatisfied. He pulled the colored cloth aside. Beneath it was the face of Sebastian Newcastle.

Callender was too stunned to relish the sight, but only for a moment. He had found the lair of the vampire in the foundations of his own house. Felicia might be anywhere, in any state, but at least her betrayer had betrayed himself. Callender chuckled at a clever ruse that had gone awry. No doubt the vampire had imagined himself ingeniously concealed; he had not realized that Callender's thirst was as ravenous as his own. Callender tossed more cotton to the floor and saw that Newcastle was naked to the waist. The sight of this nude seducer drove him into a frenzy.

There were shadows all around him, and Callender knew that the sun had set. He knew the monster might leap up and devour him. He pulled half of the broken cane out of his coat; one end was needle sharp. He needed something to strike the fatal blow, and he needed it at once. The heavy butt end of the wine bottle would do.

Callender felt his own heart beating wildly, and this helped him to select the precise spot where he should strike. He placed the jagged point against the cold, smooth skin, then smashed down with the heavy glass.

The ebony ripped through the yielding flesh, and a high-pitched wail was forced from the corpse's lips, startling Callender into striking again and again. Each blow produced a delicate moan that made his skin crawl. The death agonies were uncanny. Something was wrong.

The vampire's body began to shake. It thrashed from side to side, then crumbled like a hollow shell. Pieces of flesh dropped away. A glass eye rolled across the cellar. The skin shattered. Something was breaking free.

Shards of Newcastle flew in all directions. Most of his face came to rest beside the other face beneath it.

Felicia Lamb lay among wax fragments, the sharp shaft of Callender's broken cane embedded in her breast.

Callender wondered why she didn't bleed. He had no way of knowing that there was not a drop of blood inside her. She was as white as a marble statue. Her golden hair, unleashed as he had never seen it, spread around her head like a halo. And all about her were parts of a waxen man, the remnants of Newcastle's last cruel joke.

Callender thought he saw Felicia's lashes flutter, her lips part, her fingers reaching toward her shattered heart. Then she was still, garbed in a gown of pure white silk. She looked like a sleeping angel.

His candle flared for an instant.

Callender stared at what he had done and wondered just what had been done to him. He was a murderer twice over now, and this time he sensed that he had been lured into a trap. He wondered if Felicia had been a party to the plot, if somehow she had willed her own destruction. How else could this have happened? How else could she have been concealed in that wax effigy? He thought of New-castle and of his ancient friend, Madame Tussaud. Then he could not think at all.

Callender laughed. He could hardly help himself. He picked up the bits of wax and smashed them underfoot. He found another bottle and broke its neck against the wall, then drank from sharp glass that sliced his lips.

He heard footsteps overhead, and, knowing that they came for him, he laughed again.

They found him there, his mouth dribbling blood, beside the punctured corpse of his fiancée. The sound of his incoherent voice had drawn them to him.

There were three men in blue, one holding a lantern in his bandaged hand. Behind them came Nigel Stone, apologetically brandishing a key. The light sent shadows shimmering all over the wine cellar.

"Mr. Callender," said the chief constable. "What have you been doing to Miss Lamb?"

EIGHTEEN

The Conscientious Cousin

Mr. and Mrs. Nigel Stone sat side by side on a horsehair settee and shared a bottle of fine old sherry.

Their wedding might have been a hasty one, but, as Mrs. Stone observed, a hasty wedding was better than none at all. And furthermore, their union served to disperse the sadness that might have blighted both their lives.

"To think that I have married a hero!" chirped Mrs. Stone.

"Not really," murmured Mr. Stone. "I only let the fellows in to capture him."

"But you might have been killed!" she said.

"I suppose so. He did have the other half of that stick in his coat."

291

"I have found a brave man and inherited a fortune in the same week," said Mrs. Stone. "Was ever any woman so blessed?"

"Oh, I don't know," said Mr. Stone. "I've come home from years in the wilderness, and right away I've found a charming bride. Surely I'm the lucky one."

The bride and groom exchanged chaste kisses.

"Did you hear that Madame Tussaud will be putting poor Felicia and your cousin on display?" asked Mrs. Stone. "They are to be part of a large addition to the Dead Room. It pleases me to think that the poor girl won't be forgotten."

"Indeed," said Mr. Stone. "And she's at peace now."

"Would it be in bad taste for us to visit the display?"

"As you think best, Penelope."

Mrs. Stone took a thoughtful sip of sherry. "And what of Mr. Newcastle?" she asked. "Has he been found?"

"Not a trace of him, I'm afraid," said Mr. Stone. "I suppose he feared an investigation just like any other charlatan."

"He was no charlatan," said Mrs. Stone. "That man had power. The power to change things. I hoped that he would save Felicia from your cousin, but it was not to be."

"The police think Reggie might have done away with him as well, you know, and, of course, that's what the fool said he'd done when he shoved that stick into Felicia's heart."

"Yes," said Mrs. Stone thoughtfully. "Was there much blood?"

"What? I really didn't like to look at her, to tell you the truth. She seemed quite clean, though, but poor old Reggie had blood all over his mouth."

"Like a vampire," murmured Mrs. Stone.

"What did you say, my dear?"

"Nothing, Nigel. Had your cousin really lost his mind?"

"What other explanation could there be for such unchivalrous behavior?" Mr. Stone filled both of their glasses. "I wonder if they'll keep him in the madhouse or just take him out and hang him. I wish there were more I could do for him somehow."

"I hardly think you need concern yourself, after his barbaric treatment of my niece."

"As you say, Penelope. At least I did him one good turn."

"And what was that?"

"A small thing, really. I went back to the house the day after all that happened, and I found a packing crate in the hallway."

"A packing crate?"

"Yes, and quite a large one. It was sealed, and the labels were on it, so I took it on myself to have it sent, though heaven knows what business Reggie might have had in India."

"India?"

"It was addressed to some fellow in Calcutta. I don't remember who it was, exactly, but it looked to me like some sort of Spanish name."

"A Spanish name?" said Mrs. Stone. "Oh, dear."